William Saroyan

WILLIAM SAROYAN, the son of Armenian immigrants, was born in Fresno, California, in 1908. When his father died three years later, Saroyan's mother placed her four children in a San Francisco orphanage until she was able to earn enough to care for them and return to the close-knit Armenian community. Saroyan delivered newspapers, worked in the vineyards, read in the public library but left school at fifteen to work for the San Francisco Telegraph Company. Saroyan knew he would be a writer; his first paycheck was spent on a secondhand typewriter.

Saroyan wrote novels, a ballet, song lyrics, screenplays, several autobiographies, and plays, often casting, directing, and producing them himself, but he is best known for his short stories. In collections such as *My Name Is Aram* his glorious optimism and humor are a paean to his Armenian heritage.

In 1940 Saroyan won a Pulitzer prize for his play *The Time of Your Life* but, not believing in patronage of the arts by institutions, he refused to accept. He enlisted in the Army Signal Corps in 1943 and at that time met and married Carol Marcus, a young actress. They had two children, Aram and Lucy, but were divorced, remarried, and divorced again. Saroyan then divided his time between France and California.

A few days before his death, in 1981, Saroyan told a reporter, "Everyone has got to die but I always thought an exception would be made in my case."

YEARLING CLASSICS

Works of lasting literary merit by English
and American classic and contemporary writers

YEARLING BOOKS / YOUNG YEARLINGS / YEARLING CLASSICS
are designed especially to entertain and enlighten young
people. Charles F. Reasoner, Professor Emeritus of Children's
Literature and Reading, New York University, is consultant
to this series.

For a complete listing of all Yearling titles, write to
Dell Readers Service, P.O. Box 1045,
South Holland, IL 60473.

Mama I Love You

William Saroyan

With an Afterword by Lucy Saroyan

Published by
Dell Publishing
a division of
The Bantam Doubleday Dell Publishing Group, Inc.
1 Dag Hammarskjold Plaza
New York, New York 10017

Yearling ® TM 913705, Dell Publishing, a division of the Bantam Doubleday Dell Publishing Group, Inc.

ISBN: 0-440-40041-4

RL: 4.0

Printed in the United States of America

March 1988

10 9 8 7 6 5 4 3 2 1

W

I wrote this story for Lucy Saroyan herself—with love.

Mama I Love You

Contents

Chapter 1

Good-by, Macaroni Lane

Mama Girl came out of the bath with just the stuff on to hide a big girl a little and she said, "What time is it now?"

"Eight," I said.

"Ten minutes to?"

"No, just eight."

"Which clock?"

"All clocks. It's eight and you're late, but have you *ever* been on time?"

"I wasn't late when I had you."

"I was the one who wasn't late. You were just there."

"I know all about it," Mama Girl said, "and take my word for it, I was the one who wasn't late."

"Well, then, neither was I."

That's my birth, when Mama Girl and I first met and began to be friends. We've been friends ever since, but we have at least one big fight every day. We always make up, though. We live in the same place and go around together, except when it's something for big girls only, and then Mama Girl goes and I stay, sometimes with a sitter, sometimes with Mother Viola, who is the mother of eleven grown-up boys and girls and comes to our house on week-ends to cook and clean and look at TV.

I was waiting for Mama Girl in her bedroom to watch her dress, because she knows how. She is the best dresser I ever saw. Mama Girl is pink all over, she has red hair, and she knows all about dressing. First you take a bath in a tub, then you put powder all over, then you make up, and then you get dressed. When you've done everything, you look like a big girl. I could do it myself, but I'm still straight up and down everywhere, and very hard instead of soft. I weigh sixty pounds and Mama Girl weighs a hundred and twenty. Mama Girl is thirty-three, but she gets angry if I say so.

"I'm twenty-two, and you know it," she says.

"If you're twenty-two," I say, "then I'm not born yet, because you were twenty-four when I was born. You said so yourself."

"I was lying," Mama Girl says. "I didn't want to tell you I was thirteen when I had you, that's all."

"That's a big fat one," I say, and Mama Girl says, "You've seen a lot of women who *are* thirty-three—well, do I look like *them?*"

Well, of course she doesn't. She doesn't look like anybody else, and she herself is different every week, after she gets back from the beauty parlor. Her hair's a different color every time, and her fingernails have a different polish. Mama Girl has more kinds of lipstick and powder and other stuff like that than any other woman in the world.

Mama Girl lighted a Parliament and sat on her bed with the red velvet spread on it. She looked at me and smiled and inhaled and exhaled, and then just sat there.

"You better hurry," I said.

"No, I'm an hour late already. It'll take me half an hour

to drive there, so I might as well take my time and be *real*
late instead of a little."

"O.K."

"What's Mother Viola cooked for your supper?"

"She's not here."

"Where is she?"

"I don't know. She hasn't come yet."

"Oh, no!" Mama Girl said. "She can't do that! She
knows I'm counting on her. I told her to be sure and be
here at seven sharp. I thought she came in while I was in
the bath."

"She didn't."

"Well, who was that you were talking to?"

"Deb."

"Mrs. Schlomb's girl?"

"Deborah Schlomb."

"Since when do you two speak together like adults?"

"Do we speak like adults?"

"Yes. I thought you were speaking to Mother Viola.
Now, I've got to find out what's the matter. Why isn't she
here?"

Mama Girl picked up the telephone with the thirty-foot
cord and dialed and waited but nobody answered.

She squashed out her cigarette in the pink ashtray with
French words written in it, and then she began to think. I
always know when Mama Girl is thinking because the
excitement around her stops and everything gets different.

"What's the matter, Mama Girl?"

Mama Girl smiled a little and then she opened her arms
and I jumped in and we hugged and Mama Girl said, "My
little Frog. My pretty little Dandelion. My little Grasshopper." So I knew Mama Girl was sad. She always calls me
her little this and her little that whenever she gets sad.

She picked up the telephone again and began to dial

quickly. After a moment she began to talk in a very special kind of voice—about airplanes and schedules—and not tomorrow, *tonight*—any time tonight. I could tell whoever she was speaking to didn't know about tonight, but finally he did. She hung up and then quickly dialed again.

"Clara," she said, "I can't make it. I'm terribly sorry. Something's come up. I'm flying to New York tonight. Yes, tonight. It's an emergency. Oh, I don't know for how long. Maybe for a month, maybe for longer, maybe for less. Of course I'm taking Mrs. Nijinsky." She listened a little while and then she said, "Hold on, I'll ask her." And then she looked at me and said, "Clara would like to have you at her house for a few weeks or a month while I'm in New York, do you want to go?"

"No, *thank* you," I said, "and you *know* it. Why do you ask me if I want to go live with Clara? She calls me Mrs. Nijinsky and cheats at cards and she says I cheat."

"She's my best friend," Mama Girl said.

"She's not mine," I said. "I want to go with you."

Mama Girl said to Clara, "She says drop dead, but I think it's awful nice of you to ask her just the same. I'll phone you when I get back. Good-by."

Mama Girl hung up and began to run around finding suitcases and hollering at me to do this and do that, check the stove, the refrigerator, the back door, the other doors, and get some clothes and a toothbrush.

That's how Mama Girl and I flew to New York instead of Mama Girl going to another party and me staying home with Mother Viola.

Chapter 2

Star of Ireland

*M*ama Girl is an actress, and that's why we flew to New York. That's where the real theater is. On the airplane—which was a TWA named *Star of Ireland*—I read the name myself as I was going up the steps to the hole in the butterfly's body that the people pass through to the seats—Mama Girl said, "I've got to get a good part in a good play because I'm not getting any younger. The new season is just starting and I've got to be there to get a good part. I've been studying very hard and I know I'm ready now, not like last year when I went to New York alone and you stayed home with Auntie Bess two whole months and I read and read but didn't get one part, because I wasn't ready. But now I am, and that's why I'm taking you with me instead of asking Auntie Bess to come and stay with you again, because this time I know I'm going to get my chance, and be a big success, and when I am, I'm going to buy you a lot of new clothes and anything else you want, so you just go to sleep."

I was too excited to go to sleep. The airplane was shaking all the time and making the noise they always make, and the people were moving up and down the aisle on their way back and forth.

"My goldfish," I said. "What about my goldfish?"

Mama Girl bought me two little goldfish in two little bowls at Woolworth's one day, thirty-five cents each, and now they were alone on the dresser in my bedroom with the ten-cent packet of goldfish food beside the two bowls, and nobody to feed them.

"Those damn goldfish," Mama Girl said.

"You take that back," I said. "How can you talk that way about Boy and Girl when they are just about my best friends and I've taken care of them all year?"

"You've had them about a month. I never thought they'd live that long. I bought them because the bowls alone are worth more than thirty-five cents each."

"I don't care why you bought them. I love my goldfish, and you take that back."

"I take it back," Mama Girl said. "I'll wire Clara and ask her to look in once a week and give them a pinch of food."

"*Twice* a week."

"Twice, then."

"Don't forget."

"I won't."

"Write it down."

If Mama Girl doesn't write something down she forgets it, but sometimes she forgets stuff she writes down, too. She writes things down all day and all night. Mama Girl opened her handbag and brought out her pad and her silver pencil and she wrote *Wire Clara feed goldfish.*

"Anything else?" she said.

"Yes. Suppose you don't get your chance?"

"I wish you wouldn't ask questions like that. I've *got* to get my chance this time or it will be just too late."

"Too late for what?"

"To be a great actress."

"Aren't you *now?*"

"I am, but I haven't been in a play. I've done a little TV, but that doesn't count. Silly parts. Silly stories, silly plays, silly directors. I'm sick of TV. I've got to be in the real theater."

"Why?"

"To be famous."

"Aren't you famous now?"

"Not quite. I'm the most beautiful girl at every party, I meet all the producers and directors and writers and actors, but nobody jumps up and says he's got to have me in his play—nobody. I'm sick and tired of it. I've got to get my chance this time. And *you've* got to believe I will, because I'll get lucky if you believe."

"O.K."

"That's a good girl."

"I believe you'll get the best part of all and be ten times as famous as Marilyn Monroe."

"Some girls have all the luck."

"You *like* Marilyn, don't you?"

"Of course. She's a real nice girl, but just think how lucky she is."

"You're going to be luckier than Marilyn Monroe."

"Say a prayer, too, and then go to sleep. It's after midnight."

I closed my eyes real tight and saw a lot of orange colors, but I didn't like the noise the airplane had to make all the time to get us to New York.

"That's a good girl," Mama Girl said. "Did you pray?"

"Yes," I said, but I didn't open my eyes, because I liked watching the orange colors, and then the black ones, too.

"What did you say?"

"Let Mama Girl be famous and successful the way she wants to be, and I'll be very kind to worms."

"But you're not *unkind* to worms anyhow, are you?"

"Of course not. I've always been kind to them."

"Well, why did you say you'd be kind to them, then?"

"Oh, Mama Girl, don't you know anything about praying? I always ask for something and then promise something."

"All right. But what worms are you thinking of?"

"The ones in the garden. I never squash them. I just look at them as they wiggle away and hide again."

"Are you asleep?"

"How could I be talking if I was asleep?"

"I mean, are you *almost* asleep?"

"I guess so."

"Good night, then."

"Good night."

But I hate the noise airplanes make and the way they shake all the way to where they're going, and I didn't feel the way I do when I'm in bed and I can stretch out nice and cool, and remember stories. Most little girls hate witches. I love witches. In stories they always make everything exciting. I don't like a story without a witch. Deb says there are no witches. I say there are. We fight and don't talk sometimes for a whole afternoon, and then Deb says, "All right, there *are* witches." Or I say, "All right, there *aren't* witches, but what's the difference? There *used* to be, because they're in the best stories." And then we make up.

A real witch with a very long thin nose all covered with warts and hairs saw me and cackled. I got scared, and I knew there are witches, and fell asleep.

Chapter 3

Hello, Pierre

We took a taxi from La Guardia to the Pierre on Fifth Avenue, which is one of the best and most expensive hotels in New York, only instead of paying twenty dollars a day for a great big room Mama Girl pays three for a very little one—a room for the servants or secretaries of rich people. The rich people sleep in the big rooms.

"I don't want anybody to know I'm poor," Mama Girl said. "It's nobody's business but my own how much rent I pay."

"Where do I sleep?"

"Right there, silly."

"Where do you?"

"Right there, too."

"Oh, Mama Girl, I'm glad we came to New York!"

The whole room was no bigger than the entrance hall of our house in Pacific Palisades, but it was on the twenty-first floor, room number 2109. It had a nice bath, a nice bed, a nice bureau, a nice closet, and of course a telephone, but not a pink one, just black, and with a soft bell, not a fire-alarm bell like the bell of the pink telephone at home.

Mama Girl sat on the bed and called room service for a pot of coffee for her, and boiled eggs and toast and cocoa for me—ugh! I hate boiled eggs and love coffee, but I'm not allowed to have coffee.

Mama Girl drew a bath and said, "All right, Mrs. Nijinsky, go soak, please."

"Don't call me Mrs. Nijinsky, please."

"Well, you were dancing, weren't you?"

"I don't care. Clara Coolbaw calls me that and she hates me, so I hate her, and I don't want you to call me what *she* calls me. Call me Margaret Rose."

"All right, Margaret Rose, but take off your clothes. I want you to soak, I want you to have a nice breakfast, I want you to stretch out in bed and rest—you didn't sleep at all."

"I did too."

"Well, not well, anyhow—and neither did I. Why do you want me to call you Margaret Rose?"

"Of England of course. The Queen's little sister."

"Oh."

"You're the Queen of England, and I'm your little sister."

"Wouldn't it be wonderful if we were?"

"No, *really*, Mama, we *are*. We're just pretending to be poor."

"That's one thing we're *not* pretending," Mama Girl said.

"How do you get to be the Queen and her sister?"

"Get in the tub and soak, please—and look here, Grasshopper, you simply have got to eat more—you're all little sticks stuck together. Starting with your breakfast after your bath, from now on you're going to eat. All right?"

"I'll do my best, Mama Girl."

I got in the tub and soaked and sang while Mama Girl made phone calls. I heard her talking to different people.

With some of them she laughed and screamed and called them names, but with others she spoke like somebody else speaking. I heard the waiter push the table into the room and go, and then Mama Girl came and I got out of the tub and she dried me and I put on a robe and sat at the table. Mama Girl opened the two eggs, one brown and one white, and she put two pats of butter with them, and the butter began to melt, and she said, "All right, I want you to be a real gobbler from now on—eat everything on that table, please, and make it fast."

"Eggshells, dishes, knives and forks and spoons, too?"

"Yes."

"Napkins?"

"Yes."

"Glasses?"

"Everything, that's all, and it's no joke. A young mother is terribly criticized if her daughter doesn't look like a Kewpie doll, and you certainly don't."

"I don't want to look like a Kewpie doll."

"A young mother with nobody in the world but a little girl is *terribly criticized.*"

"You've got Papa Boy."

"No, Frog. *You've* got Papa Boy. I haven't. We're divorced."

"Well, Papa Boy ain't *dead.* He ain't dead yet, and as long as he ain't dead, I've got him, and *you've* got him, too."

"I'm afraid not. Besides, he's in Paris, and he plans to stay there for some time to come."

"He sends the money, Mama Girl."

"Yes, he does—when he can raise it."

"And you've got my brother Pete, too."

"No, your brother's with your father."

"Why did my father take my brother to Paris?"

"You know perfectly well we all agreed a year ago that your father would have Pete with him if Pete wanted to be with him—and he did—and that you would be with me if you wanted to be with me—and you did."

"I want to be with my father, too."

"Just eat your eggs."

"No, really, Mama Girl. I want to be with him and my brother Peter Bolivia Agriculture, and I want you to be with them, too."

"Well, I'm here, you're here, and your father and Pete are in Paris—and that's the end of the matter."

"Why?"

"Now, I've got a lot of things to think about, so I'm not going to try to explain something I've already tried to explain a hundred times. Your father and your mother are divorced, that's all. When a man and a woman are divorced—well, they don't live together anymore."

"You love Papa more than you love anybody else in the whole world, and you know it."

"Maybe I do, but there's nobody I *hate* more, either."

"You *don't*, Mama! You just love him."

"I hate him."

"And he loves you."

"And he hates me."

"How can you love each other and hate each other?"

"It's easy for us."

"I love my father, and I love you, Mama Girl."

"Who do you hate?"

"Pete."

"Peter Bolivia Agriculture?"

"*Yes*, Peter Bolivia Agriculture."

"You know you love him."

"I hate him."

"All right, then, you know how it is with your father

and me. Now, every bit of that toast, and every drop of that cocoa, too."

"Telephone my father and tell them both to come here."

"Here?"

"Yes, right here. In this room. Number 2109 at the Pierre. We'll all live here until we die."

"The four of us in this room—we'd be dead in an hour. When you were a little girl the four of us lived in a *twenty-room* house in Oyster Bay for six months and it nearly killed us."

"What nearly killed us?"

"Being in the same house, trying to be a family."

"Why? Is it hard to be a family?"

"It is for your father and me. I suppose it's hard for everybody, but of course I may be mistaken. All I can go by is what I see. Take my best friend, Clara Coolbaw, for instance. Well, she's been in the same house with her husband and three children for twenty years and look what it's done to them."

"What's it done to them?"

"Why, they're all dead, that's all. They keep getting up and eating and walking around, but they're dead. That's marriage for you."

Well, then the telephone rang and I couldn't ask Mama Girl to explain. I'd have to wait again.

"Gladys!" Mama Girl screamed on the phone. "Listen, it's now or never. I've got to get started in the theater. I was all set to go to another party last night when I decided the hell with it—the hell with parties forever. I'm just not going to waste my whole life being a pretty girl at parties. It's just not enough fun, that's all. So I flew here, and I'm seeing Mike McClatchey at '21' in an hour."

Mama Girl talked and talked and drank coffee and

lighted one cigarette after another because Gladys is Gladys
Dubarry, and you know who she is. Just one of the richest
girls in the whole world, that's all, and Mama Girl's best
friend, better than Clara, even, because Gladys and Mama
Girl knew each other when they were both little girls and
very unhappy.

After a long time Mama Girl and Gladys stopped talking, Mama Girl began to throw off her clothes to get in
the tub, and then she came out and got dressed. She
pushed the table out into the hall, and put me in bed, and
she gave me a book called *Early One Morning*, all about
great men and women when they were children, with
almost no pictures, and she said, "Read and rest and sleep
until I have lunch with Mr. McClatchey. I'm late, but I
ought to be there by half past two, and back here by half
past four, and then we'll make plans for tonight. All
right?"

"All right, Mama Girl. Who's Mr. McClatchey?"

"He produces plays. We met at a party a couple of years
ago, and just think, he didn't forget me."

"Nobody forgets you, Mama Girl."

"I told him I was here to go to work in the theater and
he said, 'Good for you, come to lunch and tell me all
about it.' Keep your fingers crossed."

"O.K. Good luck, Mama Girl."

Mama Girl kissed me all over my face, and then she
went, and I looked inside *Early One Morning*. There was a
drawing of a little boy holding a shell to his ear, and I
wished I had a shell like that to listen to—right now. But
I didn't, and then the telephone rang and it was Mr.
McClatchey. He said he was very sorry but he hadn't been
able to get away from his office yet so he would be late
getting to lunch. I told him it was all right because my
mother was late, too. He asked about me, and then he said,

"Well, young lady I like your voice. Do you want to be an actress?"

"No, sir," I said. "But my mother does."

"I *know* she does," he said, "but I need a little girl with a nice voice."

"My mother has a nice voice."

"Of course, but your mother isn't nine years old and you are, and the girl in the play is. You think about it, will you?"

"Yes, sir."

Oh, no. How could I ever be an actress?

Chapter 4

Early One Morning

I read poems in *Early One Morning* without understanding a word, and then I just looked at two whole pages, the way pages in a book are, like a picture. And then I shut the book and put it on the floor and got under the covers the way I do when it's night and time to sleep and I looked up at the ceiling until it wasn't a ceiling anymore.

I dreamed my mother was getting dressed for a party and all of a sudden changed her mind and decided not to go but to go to New York instead, and take me. I dreamed we got on the *Star of Ireland* and flew to New York and took a taxi to the Pierre and began to live in 2109, bathing and eating and using the telephone. I dreamed everything we had done, only now I was safe in bed and resting instead of the way it had been.

Pretty soon I stopped dreaming, but the airplane kept shaking and making noise and I wished it would stop, but it wouldn't. I kept riding in the airplane and taking the taxi and being in 2109 until I heard a key in the lock and woke up, and there was Mama Girl.

"What's the matter, Frog? You look all hot and red."

She ran and put her hand on my forehead and then ran

to the bathroom and ran back with a thermometer and stuck it in my mouth and ran to the phone and talked to somebody about a doctor, and then she talked to the doctor, and then she took the thermometer out of my mouth and read it and said to the doctor, "A hundred and three." And then she talked and listened and hung up and came and sat and held my hands and I said, "Oh, Mama Girl, I'm not sick."

"Yes, you are," Mama Girl said. "But the doctor's on his way, and he'll make you better."

"I'm *not* sick. I just can't get the airplane to stop. It keeps making all that noise."

"Where?"

"In my ears. I *know* I'm here, not on the airplane, but it won't stop."

"He'll give you some medicine. I'll cancel everything for tonight and sit here with you."

"Oh, no, Mama, I don't want you to cancel anything."

"Well, I don't care what you want, it's what I'm going to do. Now, you just lie back and rest and don't think."

The telephone rang and it was Gladys Dubarry again. Mama Girl told her all about lunch with Mr. McClatchey.

"He hasn't got a part for me," she said, "but he wants to meet Grasshopper. He likes her voice and wants to see if she's right for the little girl, but I don't know about a thing like that. I flew here to go on the stage, not to put my daughter on. I hate kids on the stage. Besides, she's got a fever. A hundred and three, but she says she's not sick. You know how kids are. They can do anything better than grownups, even be sick better. Oh, no, you don't have to send your doctor, I've got a doctor coming. Of course your doctor's the best, but it's not necessary to send him."

"Let her send him," I said. "I want to see Gladys Dubarry's doctor."

"She says she wants to see your doctor," Mama Girl said, "but will you please listen to me, Gladys, it's just a little fever, she's fine, she really is, and I don't want a lot of fuss made about her. Of course I can't take any chances, but I'm sure it's nothing serious. Why should it be *polio?* Listen, I want her to rest. I'll call you after the doctor leaves."

"Polio?" I said. "Oh, Mama Girl, am I going to die?"

"Now, look here," Mama Girl said. "Gladys Dubarry likes to dramatize things. She's been doing that all her life. She did it when she was a kid. No, you haven't got polio, and you're not going to die. *Gladys* has got polio of the soulio, that's all. She always wants to be the big generous rich girl, and it's an awful bore. *Her* doctor, as if he's the greatest in the world because he gives her a sedative whenever she's hysterical, which is always. Now, you just rest easy, and forget all about being sick."

"I'm *not* sick," I said. "You're the one who says I'm sick."

"Has the airplane stopped yet?"

"Well, a little."

"When it stops I'll know you're not sick."

"How can we get it to stop, Mama Girl?"

"The doctor'll give you some medicine to put you to sleep and it'll stop in your sleep."

The doctor was a little old man with a little smile and little hands. At first he just looked at me and smiled, and then he and I talked, and then he and Mama Girl talked, and then he said, "She's tired and keyed up."

"But aren't you going to take her temperature?"

"It isn't necessary," the doctor said, "but let's take it, anyhow. I believe it's gone down a little."

It was a hundred and one now, so I had lost two of them, whatever they are.

"She keeps hearing the airplane," Mama Girl said.

"I can understand that," the doctor said. "Well, give her half an aspirin now, and another half a little later on."

"Half an aspirin? Is that all?"

"She's just tired and excited."

"But I thought you'd want to give her a sedative."

"Half an aspirin *is* a sedative. She's a very strong girl— all bones and muscle and energy."

"She won't eat."

"Well, eating *is* a bore."

"Oh, you mustn't say that," Mama Girl said. "I'll have an awful time getting her to eat now."

"Forget it, my dear," the doctor said. "Really. She's a very strong little girl. She's almost all better already, just listening to us instead of the airplane. Why don't you have the desk send up a radio and let her listen to some soft music—or better still why don't you sing to her?"

"Me? Sing?"

"Of course. Very softly. She'll stop hearing the airplane."

"Is that all?"

"Well, if she falls asleep that'll be fine. Ask the operator not to ring the phone. Keep singing softly while she's asleep. When she wakes up, take her temperature again. If it's normal, let her get dressed, and then take her for a walk in the Park. This is a very small room, and it's long, something like the inside of an airplane."

"What shall I sing?" Mama Girl said. "I don't know very many children's songs."

"Oh, they don't have to be children's songs," the doctor said.

He broke an aspirin in half, put it in my mouth, Mama Girl handed me a glass of water, I swallowed, and the doctor put his little hands on my face and smiled and said, "Rockaby, baby." He didn't sing it, he said it, and then he said, "I often wish somebody would sing to *me* now and then."

Mama Girl looked at him as if he were very strange, and then she opened her bag and got out her money purse.

"How much is your call, Doctor?"

"My dear," the doctor said.

"No, I insist," Mama Girl said. "Doctors must be paid for their work."

"Oh, a dollar, then," the doctor said, and Mama Girl gave him a dollar bill.

"As for you," the doctor said to me, "you're not sick at all, you know."

"I know."

Mama Girl walked to the door with the doctor. They said a few things and then he went and Mama Girl came and sat and began to sing.

She sang her favorite song. The one with the words *Time goes by so slowly, and time can do so much.* And then when she didn't know any more words she hummed, and I thought it was beautiful. I thought Mama Girl was the most beautiful girl in the whole world. I thought the whole world was beautiful. The telephone rang and Mama Girl spoke quickly and softly and hung up and came back and began to sing some more.

I never felt so good in all my life.

Chapter 5

Twosies

I smelled Mama Girl and went to sleep. It was her regular smell, which is herself, a big girl, then expensive perfume, then cigarette smoke, then the smell of her clothes.

She sang and sang, sometimes with words, sometimes without, and then in my sleep I knew she was getting in bed with me. I heard her say something, and then kiss and cuddle me.

I felt perfect.

We stayed that way a long time and then I forgot, but I still knew I wasn't sick, I was happy, and felt perfect.

I began to hear soft voices, so I opened my eyes, and there was Mama Girl and Gladys Dubarry, and her own private doctor.

Gladys looked rich. *Very* rich. She was very thin, not like Mama Girl. Her whole body was just something to put expensive clothes on. She had a boy's haircut, and a boy's chest, too. She was speaking quickly with a high excited voice.

"Why, I don't understand," she said. "There's not room enough here for people even to *stand,* let alone sit down. Why, I'll speak to the manager immediately and have you moved to a penthouse suite. This is silly. You can't live in a closet. I won't have my friends treated this way."

"Now, just a minute," Mama Girl said. "I *asked* the manager for this room."

"But what in the world for?"

"The rent is three dollars, instead of twenty or thirty, that's what for."

"Oh, that's silly. How much do you need?"

"A million," I said, and Gladys turned and screamed, "Oh, Grasshopper! I'm so glad you're in New York with Mama Girl, and I'm going to give you a wonderful garden party."

She came and hugged and kissed me and I smelled *her,* too. Well, she smells all right, I guess, but she's no Mama Girl, I can tell you that. I don't know *what* she is. She's got everything except the part that's Mama Girl herself. She's got the perfume and the smell of expensive clothes and diamonds and rubies, but she hasn't got the other stuff Mama Girl's got.

The doctor took Mama Girl's wrist and held it and Mama Girl looked at him, and then at Gladys, and Gladys nodded, so I looked at the doctor again. He was tall and handsome, but *he* didn't have something, too.

"What are you taking *my* pulse for?" Mama Girl said.

"Gladys said you were sick."

"Oh, no—not *me*. My daughter, but she's all better, aren't you, Frog?"

"I feel fine," I said.

"She's been asleep almost an hour," Mama Girl said. She took her wrist away.

"I think we'd better take *your* temperature," the doctor said.

He put the thermometer in Mama Girl's mouth, and after a while he looked at it and said, "Just as I thought.

Almost a hundred and two. Well, now, what's the matter with *you?*"

"I like *that,*" Mama Girl said. "You're the doctor. Why ask me? I haven't the faintest idea."

"All right," the doctor said. "To bed, to rest, to sleep."

"To bed—here?" Gladys screamed. "The two of them in the same *cleaning-woman's* bed?"

"Oh, get off your high horse," Mama Girl said. "I've come to New York to go on the stage, not to sleep in famous beds. You sleep in some queen's, don't you?"

"Of course," Gladys said. "You must pick up your darling daughter and get out of this clothes closet immediately."

"Cut it out," Mama Girl said. "This is my home in New York, and I'll thank you to remember I didn't ask you here. I don't expect you to blab this all over New York, either. I live at the Pierre, that's all."

The door buzzed, and it was a hotel bellboy with a package for me. It was a little Indian doll with a sticker on the bottom of one foot, and on the sticker was a little stamp that said $1. The card said "To a very lovely little girl." It was from my doctor.

Gladys and Mama Girl talked and argued, and Gladys screamed and found fault with Mama Girl's room, and offered money, but Mama Girl refused, and finally Gladys and her private doctor went away.

Mama Girl told the hotel operator to let absolutely nobody ring the bell, and then she got back in bed and hugged me again and whispered and laughed and said, "Oh, Frog, first you get a fever, and then I get one, and I think we're both dying."

"I don't care if we are," I said. "I like it."

Pretty soon Mama Girl fell asleep, and I just watched her and listened to her breathing.

It got nice and quiet. I heard automobile horns softly,

and other sounds, street voices, and the whistles traffic cops blow, but not the airplane.

I tried to hear the airplane again but I couldn't, I could only remember hearing it and the way I felt when I heard it, but I couldn't feel the way I *had* felt anymore.

I couldn't stop feeling perfect.

I was in bed with Mama Girl and she was asleep. I was awake, and it was twosies: Mama Girl and me.

It was the two of us and the whole world. It was a big round girl and a little straight one, and I loved her. I loved every bit of her. I even loved the cigarette part of the smell of her, which most of the time I didn't. I looked at her and smelled her and loved her. I touched her and loved her. Mama Girl almost smiled when I put my fingers on her lips, and then she brought her hand up slowly and took my hand, but she didn't squeeze, so I knew she was sound asleep—but she knew it was me just the same.

I got out of bed because it was too hot, and I went looking around 2109, our home in New York, which Gladys Dubarry lifted her nose at—but what does she know about anything? What does she know about not having six million dollars, and having only six maybe, or sixty, or at the very most six hundred?

Still, it *was* a small room. I loved it, though. I loved every bit of it, because it kept Mama Girl and me close together, but I opened the door to see what there was to see, and of course it was a hall. I went down the hall, and then I heard the door slam. I ran back but the door was locked from the inside and I couldn't get in. I didn't want to wake Mama Girl, but I had to do something. I hadn't expected the door to close. Now I heard the elevator stop. I heard the door open. I heard footsteps, and I got ashamed, but there was no place to hide. Pretty soon a very tall lady carrying packages came around the corner and said, "Young lady, please help me with these packages and I'll ask you in to tea."

"Yes, ma'am," I said.

I reached up and took four of the small packages. We walked all the way to the end of the hall, and the lady put a key into the lock and turned the key and pushed the door open, and we went in. She plopped her packages on a low glass table, so I did, too. She sat down and sighed, and then she said, "Well, now, let me have a look at you."

She looked at me straight up and down, and then she said, "Will you turn around, please?" So I did, and then she said, "You're awfully skinny, but there's something about you I like. Is there anything about me that *you* like?"

I said, "Yes," and the lady said, "Well, all right now, don't keep me on tenterhooks—what is it?"

"Well," I said, "I don't know."

"It's the same with adults, only it's the other way around—they *don't* like me, and don't know why. Where do you live?"

"One thousand and one Macaroni Lane, Pacific Palisades."

"How'd you get *here?*"

"Airplane."

"Where's your father?"

"Paris."

"Where's your mother?"

"2109."

"Isn't that the little room up the hall?"

"Yes."

The lady thought a moment and then she said, "Well, then, look here—let's have a cup of tea."

"O.K."

Chapter 6

The Dragnet for the Tea Drinker

*T*he tall lady had a sliver teapot and tray and sugar and creamer and slop bowl, a *whole* set, with roses and rose leaves carved in the silver, and very thin cups and saucers that you could almost see through.

She drank tea strong, with only a little lemon in it—a very thin slice, which she ate, peel and all.

For me she put a little tea in the bottom of a cup and then all the rest was cream. I liked it very much. It tasted better than cream alone, which I hate. She had a whole plate loaded with all kinds of store cookies, or biscuits, as she called them, and then she had a cake straight from a famous baker's—soaked in rum. She had a small piece, and she let me have a small piece, too.

I liked the tea, and some of the cookies, but best of all I liked the rum cake—I liked the wet cool flavor in there.

While we were drinking and eating the lady talked as if she were my own age and we were pretending to be having tea, from a play set. I kept noticing how like Deborah Schlomb she sounded, and then I kept noticing where we were, in one of the finest apartments at the Pierre, with a lot of the furniture brought in by the lady herself, most likely, her own stuff, certainly the fine paintings on the wall, two of her, two of children, so I knew she wasn't my age, and *was* Somebody. Somebody nice, too, nicer than anybody I had ever met, anybody I had ever *heard* about, even.

We made a lot of conversation, we drank tea and ate cookies and rum cake, we laughed, and the time went by. Mama Girl was fast asleep and she *needed* to sleep. I was all better. I could get back to 2109 in a jiffy, so of course I didn't give the matter of going back a lot of thought. I *should* have, though.

I guess Mama Girl woke up. What woke her up, I don't know. Maybe she could smell that I was out of the room. Anyhow, she must have thought at first that I was hiding, because we do that a lot, sometimes I hide, sometimes she hides, and we find each other. Well, I guess she didn't get out of bed, just lay there and talked, and she believed I heard her, but of course I didn't, because I wasn't there, I was down the hall having tea and rum cakes with the tall lady. So then, I guess, Mama Girl said to me to come out of the closet, or the bathroom, or from under the bed, or from behind the end of the bureau, or from any place in the room where I could hide, but of course I wasn't there. So then, I guess, Mama Girl got out of bed to find me, and began to look, and of course *didn't* find me. And then she got scared. She begged me not to hide anymore, to please come out, and then she just happened to look at the window of 2109 and of course it was open from the bottom for ventilation, not all the way open, but halfway, and she screamed, and began to run around half crazy. She tried to calm down and then got the manager on the line and talked very calmly and told him everything. The manager had the assistant manager speak to the desk, and the desk spoke to the bellboys, and so a search was started for me. The manager himself went out into the street to have a look, and of course everything was the same as ever out there. He told Mama Girl she had given him one of the worst scares of his whole career in the hotel business. Little girls just don't fall out of the Hotel Pierre, he said.

I was drinking more tea and eating more rum cake when I began to hear walking up and down in the hall, but I didn't think it had anything to do with me. It did, though. It was bellboys, and the male house detective and the female house detective. They stopped at 2109 first and talked to Mama Girl, who showed them a photograph of me, and then they began walking in the hall. The dragnet was out.

Finally, the female detective buzzed the tall lady's door. The lady asked me to please see who it was, so I did, but when I opened the door the female detective jumped and made a funny little noise, and the lady said, "All right, now, who is it?"

The female detective said who it was, which annoyed the tall lady.

"Well, what do you mean buzzing *my* door?" she said.

"A little girl has been lost out of 2109."

"Who says so?"

"Her mother."

"Oh, oh," I said. "I've got to go."

There just wasn't time to say a polite thank you and good-by. I was out the door, past the female D., and up the hall to 2109 in no time at all. But the door was shut. I wanted to get inside as quickly as possible, because there were bellboys all around, and all I had on was a pink nightgown that you could almost see through. I knocked quickly and said, "Mama Girl."

The door opened like an explosion. Mama Girl took

one look at me and just let out all the air in her in one big terrible sigh. She didn't say a word. She just went back to bed. I went in and closed the door after me and went to her and said I was sorry and she said I shouldn't have gone off and that I had scared her half to death, and would I please lift the telephone and ask for the manager and tell him I wasn't lost any more but back in 2109 with my mother, which I did.

Then she got all the way under the covers, with the covers over her head.

I was sorry to see Mama Girl under the covers that way, because she does that only when she's very unhappy, and I was the one who had made her unhappy. I said, "Oh, Mama Girl, please don't be unhappy, please don't hide from me, I'm sorry." Only Mama Girl didn't come out from under the covers She just said something, only I didn't know what.

"What did you say, Mama Girl?"

"I said you've made an awful fool of me."

"Oh, no, Mama Girl, I haven't at all. Please come out."

"No. I'm mad. I'm mad at you. I'm mad at your father. I'm mad at Peter Bolivia Agriculture. I'm mad at Clara Coolbaw and Gladys Dubarry—but most of all I'm mad at Mother Viola, because if she had come at the proper time I wouldn't have come to New York, and now that I'm in New York, I wish I were back in California."

"Oh, no, this is best."

"It's *worst.* I wish I was dead."

"Oh, Mama Girl, don't say that—it's bad luck. God will hear you and believe you and take you to Heaven, and then where will I be?"

"Out in the hall on the twenty-first floor of the Pierre,"

Mama Girl said. "What in the world did you do a silly thing like *that* for?"

"Oh, please come out."

"No. I'm mad. Go away."

"Where shall I go?"

"Go to Paris. Go to your father. But don't you dare go in your nightgown. A divorced mother takes a lot of criticism. People would say I wasn't bringing you up right."

"Oh, but you *are*, Mama Girl."

"You bet your life I am, sick as I am."

"Are you *still* sick?"

"Sick as a dog. *Dying* sick. *Heartbroken* sick."

"Oh, what's the matter, Mama Girl?"

"I'm a failure. I'm nobody. I'm nothing."

"You, Mama Girl? Oh, no. You're a success. You're Somebody. You're Everything."

Mama Girl came out suddenly and said, "Do you really think so, Frog?"

"*Think* so?" I said. "I *know* so. You're the most beautiful and most successful girl in the whole world."

"All right, then, we'll both get dressed and go for a walk."

"Yay."

"Not so loud. This isn't school. It's the Pierre. A divorced mother gets criticized."

"Soft yay."

"Yes, Frog, keep the yays soft."

"Softer yay."

"Lovely."

"Softest yay."

"Beautiful."

I said a yay so soft Mama Girl said, "What did you say?"

"Yay."

"Yes, but softer, Frog. Now, we'll wear matching dresses, all right?"

"Yay."

"Softer. The blue ones all spattered with red and white flowers?"

"Soft yay."

We got dressed and we were both all better again, all rested, and it was almost nighttime in New York now, and we were there. We were there together instead of together in the house on Macaroni Lane in Pacific Palisades.

Yay.

Chapter 7

New York, New York

When we got in the elevator to go down to the lobby the elevator boy, who was really a man of fifty or sixty, or maybe seventy or eighty, looked at us, because Mama Girl is always so beautiful, and maybe even because I looked all right, too.

When the elevator stopped and a man and his wife got in, *they* looked at us, too, and then the woman began to whisper to the man. I watched them both, and it seemed to me the man wanted to turn around and look at us again, but he didn't dare, and then the woman did—but just a little. Mama Girl was waiting for her, and looked at her real straight, the way she does when she thinks somebody is being rude on purpose. Mama Girl doesn't get mad when somebody is accidentally rude or doesn't know any better, but when it's on purpose, she gets *very* mad. The elevator stopped again and this time two men and two women got in. They were happy and laughing, the way people are who have been having a nice time. They noticed Mama Girl and me, and they were very nice about us without saying anything or turning to look again, but the man who was with the whispering woman turned and looked at Mama Girl again, and I knew Mama Girl was going to say something, so I squeezed her hand very hard, and she looked down and smiled and lifted her eyebrows. I knew that meant *All right, all right, I won't say anything, but some people who live at the Pierre act as if they were living over a stable.*

The elevator stopped again, and this time three more people got in, strangers to one another, and quiet about getting in. Everybody moved back toward us to make room.

It stopped once more and two more people got in, and then there just wasn't any more space in the elevator, so when the elevator operator began to stop at another floor, one of the men who was happy said, "All right now, Joe, let's not try to get everybody in New York in. We're a nice cozy crowd, so let's not spoil it."

Mama Girl laughed, and I laughed, but the whispering woman looked at the man who had spoken as if he were silly.

The elevator operator stopped the elevator and opened the door again, and this time all there was out there was one old man with a turned-up mustache and a walking stick. He just looked at the crowd in the elevator and waved at the operator to move along without him, but the elevator operator waited for him to get in, and he said, "Going down, please."

"You've got enough passengers," the man said. "I'll catch the next elevator."

"Only one running just now," the elevator operator said.

"I'll wait," the man said.

"Better get in now. Plenty of room."

"I can't stand crowds—go along."

But the elevator operator *wouldn't* go along. He just waited. The buzzer buzzed some more and the operator looked at the different floors that were waiting, and he said, "I got a lot of people waiting. Get in."

This made the man angry. He even lifted his walking stick.

"Now you listen to me," he said. "Shut that door and go along."

But the elevator operator didn't shut the door.

The four people who were happy and laughing got out of the elevator together, and the other man—the one who *hadn't* said anything so far—said, "I've always wanted to walk around on the eleventh floor of the Pierre, so this is my chance. Please tell room service to send up a bottle of champagne and four glasses. We'll be down the hall here." He turned to the man with the walking stick. "You are entirely right. We have been tyrannized by elevators and elevator operators long enough. I say, 'Down with elevators.' " He turned to the operator and said, "Down, sir."

The elevator operator slammed the door shut. I was sure we would go all the way down this time, but instead we began to go up, and everybody looked at everybody. We picked up some people on nineteen, some more on sixteen, and then we dropped to nine, and there the whole car got jammed with people—and *then* at last the elevator went all the way down to the lobby floor.

The people got out, and then Mama Girl and I got out, too.

All the bellboys looked at us, and when we stepped to the desk the man there looked at us, and so did some other people behind the desk. They looked first at Mama Girl, and then at me, and then they all smiled.

The whispering woman said to the man at the desk, "I believe your elevator operator has gone mad." She went off quickly, followed by her husband.

The man at the desk said, "Is anything the matter in the elevator?"

Mama Girl said, "He needs a little help, and some of the people are having a little fun, that's all."

The man said, "He's one of our oldest employees." And then he looked at me again and then at Mama Girl and he said, "I see you've found your daughter."

"Yes, thank you."

"I understand she was visiting Miss Cranshaw."

"Who?"

"Miss Kate Cranshaw."

"The actress?"

"Well, she's been retired for some time. She only teaches now."

"I thought she was dead."

"Oh, no. She's had the north penthouse on the twenty-first floor for years, and she's far from dead, I can tell you that."

"Who does she teach?"

"The stars, of course."

"Stage?"

"Stage, screen, television, and everything else."

"Thank you," Mama Girl said, and we went down the long lobby to Fifth Avenue.

"Dandelion," Mama Girl said, "do you know who you visited?"

"Who?"

"The greatest acting coach in the world, that's all. Miss Kate Cranshaw."

"What does she do?"

"She teaches actors how to act."

"Don't actors know how to act?"

"Oh, no. The best actors keep learning all the time. Now, I want you to tell me all about Miss Cranshaw."

"What about her?"

"Well," Mama Girl said, "do you think she'd like me?"

"She liked me, so she'll like you, too. You're my mother. Of course I didn't have very many clothes on when we met."

"Was she shocked?"

"Oh, no. She didn't even notice."

"She's a lady, that's all. Now, listen, Frog, I want you to tell me all about her."

"She's very tall. Very skinny. Very elegant. She's got very sharp eyes. She speaks very clearly, and she's a lot of fun."

"What else?"

Mama Girl and I walked down Fifth Avenue and I tried to tell her all about Kate Cranshaw, but of course I never knew that's what her name was. She didn't ask mine and didn't tell me hers.

We walked on the Park side of Fifth Avenue.

"Smell them?" Mama Girl said.

"Smell what?"

"The trees of Central Park, Frog. The grass of Central Park. The birds and squirrels of Central Park."

"I smell them, I guess."

"When we come to an entrance we'll go in and then you'll *really* smell them—and the people, too."

After about a block we came to an entrance, and walked into Central Park. Pretty soon we were off the boulevard in the Park that was crowded with automobiles. We were on a path that was only for walking people, not even for people on bicycles. There we stopped, and Mama Girl looked at the trees and the big slabs of black rock in the earth, and the bushes with blossoms, and the lawn.

She breathed deeply.

"I love Central Park," she said.

"I do, too. Why do *you?*"

"Because it's in New York."

"If you love New York, why don't you *live* in New York?"

"I hate New York."

"Oh, Mama Girl, I wish you wouldn't talk that way. You love, you hate."

"But it's true, Grasshopper. Of course I love New York. Of course I hate New York."

"Why?"

"Because that's the way it is. That's the way it *really* is. That's the way nobody wants to say it is, but that's the way it is. I've known this Park from long before I could even talk. I love it and I hate it, and I wish the whole world were better."

"Than what?"

"Than what it is."

"What is it?"

"All mixed up and very sad."

"It is *not.* It's *happy.*"

"All right, happy. Don't you see, Frog, I'm scared?"

"What about?"

"Me. The way I live. The way I've lived for so long. The way I do things. The way I've made a mess of my whole life, every one of my thirty-three years."

"Thirty-three? You're twenty-one, Mama Girl."

"Oh, Frog, you're my friend, my best friend, but I *am* scared."

"Don't be, Mama Girl."

"I'm scared you're going to live the kind of life I've lived, because I'm your mother and you spend so much time with me."

"I *want* to live that way."

"It's no good, Frog."

"What *is?*"

"That's just it. I don't know. I wish I did. Nobody I know knows, either. We're all unhappy about our lives, but we don't know what to do about it. Yesterday at this time we were in California. So where are we now?"

"Here. In beautiful Central Park."

"What for?"

"So you can go on the stage and be famous."

"Oh, I make me sick, Frog. Do you know, I don't think I've got any acting ability at all?"

"Oh, you're a *great* actress, Mama Girl."

"To *you,* maybe."

"And I'm not easy to please, either, you know. If you weren't a great actress, you'd never be able to fool me. I'd know. You'll get a great part, wait and see."

"But I had lunch with the best producer in the theater, and he just *didn't* offer me a part—not even a little tiny part—and he's having us to breakfast tomorrow morning, so he can meet *you.* Frog, do you want to go on the stage?"

"Oh, no. I don't know how to act. I'm too little to act."

"He wants you to act a little girl—a girl like yourself—so of course you won't have to try, or anything. All you'll have to do is remember things to say and do."

"I don't want to."

"Are you sure?"

"Mama Girl, do you *want* me to act?"

"I don't know. I'm confused. I've always hated mothers who make their children act, who live off what their children earn, who turn their children into little monkeys—but now I don't know. I certainly don't want to *keep* you from a wonderful life."

"Where?"

"In the theater."

"Where will you be?"

"Oh, I'll be in the background somewhere, like all the other mothers with little monsters on the stage."

"Mama Girl!"

"Oh, I don't mean *you*, Frog. I mean the poor mothers and their poor unhappy children. I hate the whole idea of having children in the theater, but then there *are* a lot of fine plays that *have* got to have children in them, and *somebody* has got to play them. I don't know."

We came to a bench that nobody was sitting on, so we sat on it. I took Mama Girl's little hand, almost as little as my own, and I held it tight, because she was very unhappy, and I didn't want her to be.

Chapter 8

The Crazy Hummingbird of Central Park

*I*t was very hot in New York, even in Central Park, even in the late afternoon. While we were sitting on the bench I saw a bush with long yellow blossoms, and then I saw a hummingbird put his long beak, like a needle, into a blossom and just stay there a moment, his wings going so fast all you could see was a blur. And then I saw the hummingbird jump straight up as if he'd been scared by something, but I guess he hadn't been, because after he got up there he just slipped very quickly to another blossom, and again he put his beak in and stayed there, taking the perfume out of the blossom. He didn't stay long, though. Again he went off very quickly, as if he just had to, and knew what he was doing. But this time instead of going straight up, he went straight out, stopped a moment, and then dived on a new blossom.

Why did he go one way and not another? The bush was covered with blossoms. They were all over. Could he smell which ones had the most perfume to take?

Again the hummingbird whizzed away, this time to the other side of the bush, almost out of sight, but I could still see some of him, his tail, and it was going the same as his wings.

He was a beautiful little thing, but how could he keep going so fast all the time? Didn't he ever stop? Well, then he did, he stopped. He stood with his own two feet, like any other bird, on a bare twig of the bush—and everything stopped moving. He just stood, and I *saw* him, and he was only a very small bird now, with a long beak. He wasn't the swift fellow he'd been a moment ago. But he didn't stand long. He stood about as long as it takes to count three, and then he went to work again, going this way and that, and every time swiftly, wildly, in a way I couldn't understand.

I squeezed Mama Girl's hand. She looked at me, and then she said, "What is it, Frog?"

"The hummingbird. Look at him."

"Where?"

"Right there, in that bush with the long yellow blossoms."

Mama Girl looked and then she said, "Oh, isn't he beautiful? Oh, I love them."

"Isn't he a little crazy?"

"How do you mean?"

"Well, watch him. He goes this way all of a sudden, then stops, drinks a little more perfume, and then all of a sudden he's off as if something had scared him, but nothing has, and all he does is stop again and drink from another blossom. Why doesn't he take them one by one right where they are instead of jumping this way and the other?"

"He must have reasons," Mama Girl said.

She watched a long time, and then she said it again.

"Are you sad, Mama Girl?"

"Oh, no, Frog. It's disgraceful the way I make you worry about me. Of course I'm not sad. Are you?"

"Yes."

"That's good, because I'm supposed to make you happy when you're sad, so what would you like?"

"Just to be sad."

"Don't you want to be happy?"

"If the whole world is mixed up and sad—and *you* are, too—then I want to be, too."

"But you mustn't *try* to be. It's got to happen by itself."

"Nothing happens by itself."

"Sadness does."

"Not for *me* it doesn't. I've got to keep trying."

"Then you're not really sad."

"Well, I wasn't a little while ago. But I am *now.*"

"How did you manage?"

"The hummingbird, Mama Girl. I pretended to be the hummingbird. At first it was very nice, very swift and free, and I felt fine. But after a while I got tired of being so small and so busy and so crazy. I got tired of shooting off this way, and then the other. I got tired of drinking perfume out of long yellow blossoms. I got tired of everything, and that's when I began to be sad. Pretty soon I was *very* sad."

"Well, I guess you *can* be sad on purpose."

"I'm going to try to stop being sad on purpose, too."

"How?"

"Well, I'm going to say to myself I am *not* a hummingbird, so I don't *have* to be sad."

"That's a good way."

"Now I'm not sad, but I think I want to be sad again."

"Oh, you," Mama Girl said. "Let's go eat somewhere. How about the Automat?"

"Sure, but not yet."

"When?"

"Not until it's dark."

"Frog, it doesn't get dark in August until eight o'clock—not *really* dark until half past."

"What time is it now?"

"Five minutes to eight."

"All right, I don't want to eat until it's *all* dark."

"You just don't want to eat, period."

"I do."

"What do you want to eat?"

"Soup."

"Why soup all of a sudden?"

"Vegetable soup."

"All right, vegetable soup—but why, though?"

"I love soup, especially vegetable."

"If you like vegetable soup so much, why haven't you ever told me? There are all kinds of wonderful vegetable soups I could have bought for you at the grocer's. Why haven't you told me?"

"I didn't think you wanted me to. It isn't much to say, is it?"

"It's a *lot* for *you* to say, Grasshopper. Maybe if you start having a lot of soup you'll put on a little weight."

Little by little all of the light of the day went away and it was dark. So then Mama Girl said, "All right? Can we go eat now?"

"All right," I said, so we got up and began to walk out of the Park.

Chapter 9

Oh Pigeons, Oh People, Oh Little Boy

Summertime nighttime in New York is the best time of all, better than nighttime anywhere else. It's hot. Even in the dark the whole place is hot, the sidewalks are hot, the buildings are hot, the people are hot, and you can *see* how hot some of them are. Their faces show it, and so does the way they walk or stand and wait.

Across the street from the Park on the corner at Seventh Avenue there was a man with a pushcart who was standing and waiting. He was very hot. He brought a big blue handkerchief out of his back pocket and wiped his whole face dry with it. When he was finished he saw Mama Girl and me, and he said, "Buy the little girl something."

Mama Girl stopped to see what he had, and it was peanuts in their shells, sunflower seeds, pine nuts, and three or four kinds of candies.

"Well," Mama Girl said, "it's a little hot for these things, but let me see. What would you like, Dandelion?"

"Oh," I said, because I really didn't know. I really

didn't want anything he had, but I didn't want to disappoint him. I looked at everything, but everything looked hot and tired, and I really couldn't decide. At last, though, I made up my mind to have Mama Girl buy something from the man, because he was so hot and had the pushcart and all the hot things on it, and it was nighttime, and he was far away from somewhere different. He wasn't from New York, he was from somewhere else.

"Some of these," I said.

"Yes," Mama Girl said. "They're nice."

"Pine nuts," the man said. "Five cents? Ten cents?"

"Well, ten cents," Mama Girl said. The man took a little shovel and pushed it into the tray of pine nuts, and then he poured them out of the shovel onto a little scale and weighed ten cents' worth. Then he poured them into a little paper sack and twisted the ends of the sack shut. Mama Girl handed him a dime and he handed me the paper sack, and because he was from far away I said *merci* instead of thank you. He looked at me and nodded his head. Mama Girl smiled, and we went along. I twisted the ends of the sack open and let some of the pine nuts slide out of the sack into my hand and offered them to Mama Girl. She took three or four, and left five or six. I put one in my mouth and cracked it with my teeth, and then I got the shell out of the way and let it fall into my other hand, and then I ate the nut. It had a nice taste, but it was hot. Mama Girl ate one, too.

"I guess they're for canaries," she said.

"Oh, no."

"Well, they're awfully small, and you'd have to get a hundred of them out of their shells before you could have a mouthful."

"Who *wants* a mouthful?"

"Not *you*, of course," Mama Girl said. "What's good enough for a canary is good enough for you."

"They don't eat pine nuts, only people do."

We were cracking and eating them one by one as we walked up Seventh Avenue toward Fifty-seventh Street, to where Carnegie Hall is. Every time we dropped the shells on the sidewalk one or two of the sidewalk pigeons of New York would half run and half fly to them, look and peck at them, and find nothing to eat after all their trouble, so I dropped them three or four whole ones, but the pigeons couldn't get them open.

"See," I said. "Even pigeons can't eat pine nuts."

I stopped, and two pigeons stopped and looked up to see what I was going to do.

I cracked one nut, and then one more, and then I dropped the inside to them, and they gobbled them up and asked for more, so I did it again. Mama Girl did it, too, and before we knew it we had a crowd of twenty or thirty pigeons all wanting cracked pine nuts. They were all kinds, white, black, gray, and mixed, and all sizes, some big and some medium and some small, and all of them hungry and very swift on their feet, but nowhere near as swift as the hummingbird.

They were swift like people in a crowd, on their feet, and very watchful and full of looking around and up and down and all about.

Some people stopped, too. People in the streets like to stop to watch things. If nothing's happening in the streets they watch things in store windows.

There was a man with his boy. They were holding hands, but the boy got his hand free, and his father watched him go to the crowd of pigeons to catch one. He was a very little boy who wasn't too good at walking yet, but he wanted to catch a pigeon just the same. The

pigeons had had that happen to them so many times that
they were almost used to it. They let him get quite near,
and then they moved quickly, so he couldn't grab them.
At the same time they stayed near enough to scramble for
any more pine nuts Mama Girl and I happened to drop.
The father of the little boy watched a moment, and then
he went to the boy and took him by the hand.

"Don't scare the birds," he said.

The boy looked at him as if he didn't understand, and
then he said, "My birds."

I guess he meant he could go after them and catch them
or even scare them, since they were his birds.

"No," the man said, "they're *not* yours."

"Whose?" the boy said.

"Nobody's."

"No," the boy said. "My birds."

"O.K.," the man said, "Your birds, but don't scare
them."

They held hands and stood and watched a little longer,
and then they went on down the street slowly, talking and
looking back. He was a good man, and a good father to
his little boy. He reminded me a little of my father when
he used to take me walking.

Mama Girl cracked six or seven pine nuts but kept the
insides of them, and then she kneeled and held her hand
out to the pigeons to see if they would eat out of her
hand. This made a big commotion among them because
they wanted what Mama Girl had in her hand but they
weren't sure they could have it. They looked and walked
around and came near and went away, and came back,
and pretty soon one of them came straight up to Mama
Girl's hand and took one pine nut, and then he took
another. And then another pigeon came up, and the first
pigeon turned on him and drove him off. And then

another came up, and he drove him off, too, and the people who were watching laughed.

The man with the little boy came back, and now the little boy had a bag of pine nuts, too. He dropped them to the pigeons whole, and they couldn't do anything with them. The little boy's father went around and stepped on each of the little pine nuts, and then the pigeons began to peck among them for the stuff they wanted to eat. The little boy was thrilled with his father. He learned the trick of stepping on them, but after he had stepped on them they were still unbroken because he was so light.

This made him angry, so he began to stamp on them, and then he slipped and fell, and that made him so mad he began to bawl. I ran and picked him up. He said a lot of things, but he didn't stop bawling, so I couldn't understand anything he said. His father went around stepping on the unbroken pine nuts for the boy, and then he took him, and said, "Thank you, little girl." He looked at Mama Girl and said, "I don't think he's ever going to forget this experience."

Mama Girl smiled but didn't say anything, and we moved on to Fifty-seventh Street.

"Where's the little boy's mother?"

"Who knows?" Mama Girl said.

"Wasn't he a funny little boy?"

"Yes, he was."

"Wasn't his father nice?"

"Yes, he was."

"He reminded me a little of my father."

"Not at all," Mama Girl said. "Your father would have bought a dozen bags, dropped them all at once, stepped on all of them quickly, and then he would have tossed them a handful of coins, too."

"What for?"

"Your father does things like that."

"What for, though?"

"It amuses him."

"Money for pigeons?"

"He gets a kick out of doing unexpected things."

"Did you ever *see* him throw money to pigeons, Mama Girl?"

"No, but I've seen him do a lot of other things just as unexpected."

"Like what?"

"Well, let's go sit down in the Automat, and I'll see if I can remember something."

Chapter 10

The Hunger Rush
at the Automat

We crossed Fifty-seventh Street to Carnegie Hall. There was a whole crowd of people there, on the sidewalk, on the steps going up to the lobby, and a lot more were arriving by taxi, limousine, and subway. Half a block away, on Seventh Avenue, it was pigeons, a man with a pushcart, a father and his little boy, and peace and quiet, but at Carnegie it was all hurry, talk, and excitement.

"What is it?"

"A concert," Mama Girl said.

"Piano?"

"No, it's too hot for serious music. Jazz. Piano of course, but blues, Dixieland, boogie woogie, and things like that. They're fun, but not in Carnegie."

"Where, then?"

"Oh, in a honky-tonk somewhere. A saloon. A little dark room in Greenberg Village."

"Greenwitch?"

"Grennitch is the way to say it, but I once overheard a girl on a bus call it Greenberg, and I like that better. But not the piano alone—cornets, clarinets, trombones, saxophones, but especially drums. The music of the people."

"Us?"

"No, we're not the people. We *never* are. It's always somebody else."

"Let's go listen to the music of the people, whoever they are."

"No," Mama Girl said, "everybody's too thrilled about it when it comes to Carnegie, and that spoils it. Besides, we've got to have some food, and then we've got to get home and go to bed. We're both a lot more tired than we know. We've certainly been under the weather, and maybe we still are. And we've got to be fresh for breakfast tomorrow morning with Mike McClatchey. Now, please, Frog, have a nice supper, will you?"

"All right, Mama Girl."

"Soup, hot chocolate, and anything else you like."

"Ice cream."

"All right."

The Automat on Fifty-seventh Street is a good one, but you couldn't even find a space in the revolving door. When a space arrived and you went to get into it somebody would get in ahead of you and push away. Mama Girl and I watched and waited, but it looked as if we just weren't ever going to get in. Then a big man in rough work clothes took hold of the door and put his big hairy arm out to hold back the people. He nodded to me to get into a space, so I did. He pushed the door around a little, and then he nodded to Mama Girl, and she got in, too, and then he pushed the door around slowly, and we were in at last.

We turned to thank him through the glass, but we saw him walking away. There was a kind of angry expression on his face. The door began to turn very quickly now, and all kinds of people began to tumble out of the turning door. It was almost like a mechanical game of some kind that you might watch on a stage or in a circus.

There were a lot of people crowding around the change booth, too, and Mama Girl looked a little discouraged.

"The soup's so good here," she said. "And it *is* fun, isn't it?"

Well, of course it *was* fun, but it was awfully swift and a little crazy, too. It was like the sidewalk pigeons gathered together for pine nuts.

"Oh, yes, Mama Girl, it's a *lot* of fun."

"Would you rather we went somewhere else?"

"Oh, no. Let's *try*, at least."

Mama Girl opened her handbag, but just then a very large woman bumped her. The bag fell out of her hands, and I grabbed it just in time to keep *all* the things from spilling out of it and rolling away. While I was bent over, somebody bumped *me*, too. I almost lost my balance, but not quite. I got up quickly, I had the bag, and only two or three things had fallen out of it. Mama Girl found two of them—a compact and a lipstick—but she got bumped two or three times, too. And then a boy came running up with the third thing—a little comb with a silver frame around it.

"Oh, thank you very much," Mama Girl said, and then she tried to get out of the way of the hungry people, but you just couldn't. They were there, and there were more coming all the time. The boy who had brought the comb got bumped two or three times, and then at last he got to a safe place and Mama Girl held out a quarter to him, but he shook his head, and went a little farther away. He was a dark boy of eleven or twelve, and he reminded me a little of my brother Peter Bolivia Agriculture, especially when he shook his head and moved away.

At last Mama Girl got two dollars' worth of small coins, and we went to where the trays and silver and paper napkins are. We got one tray for both of us, and the other stuff, and then we waited for our turn to tell one of the girls what we wanted.

"There are three soups," Mama Girl said. "Vegetable, chicken rice, and bean."

"You know what I want."

"Vegetable," Mama Girl said. "I'll have chicken rice."

After a few minutes one of the girls poured vegetable and then chicken rice soup into two bowls. She placed a small packet of salt crackers beside each bowl, and then she got two dishes of chocolate ice cream, and then Mama Girl dropped money into a glass cage with a handle beside it, and the girl there looked at the money, and then she pulled the handle down, and the money dropped into a metal box and disappeared.

We went to where you put two nickels into a slot and a cup under a spout and pull a handle and hot chocolate comes out of the spout into the cup. I did my own, and Mama Girl did her own, but just as she was lifting her cup to place it on our tray a man bumped her arm and a lot of the hot chocolate splashed over the top of the cup onto the saucer, and then over the top of the saucer.

Now all we had to do was find a table with two places. Every table in the Automat has four places, but we just couldn't find one with two free places. We found quite a few with one place, so at last Mama Girl sat me down at a table with one free place, and then she sat down at the next table. We weren't at the same table, but we were near together. Mama Girl smiled and nodded.

I picked up my tablespoon because I knew Mama Girl was waiting to watch me eat, and I began to eat the soup. It was very good, too, but everything was so swift all around that it wasn't easy to believe I was having my supper. It was more as if I were in a big game but didn't know what the rules were.

There was a very fat man at my table, and with him was his wife, and she was just as fat as he was, and their daughter, who was my age, I guess, and she was very fat, too. I saw Mama Girl looking at the fat girl every once in a while, as if she wanted me to notice her and to eat the way she was eating, but of course I couldn't *help* noticing her and the way she was eating, which was swift and loud. She had a whole big plate covered with baked beans, mashed sweet potatoes, baked macaroni, and a big piece of baked hamburger with gravy. Her mother and father had plates just like hers, as if they had all agreed to share and share alike. They ate so quickly that I was ashamed to look at them, or afraid maybe. I was afraid they would notice me watching and bawl me out. When I was half finished with the vegetable soup their plates were all clean, and they were just sitting there very unhappy about not having anything more to gobble up. I could tell they were still hungry and I just wished I could call out to somebody and say, "All right, now, fill these plates again, please." But of course all I could do was hope they wouldn't notice me watching them, as I tried not to, and then bawl me out, because I hate to get bawled out. I just never know what to say back.

Without saying a word, the father got up suddenly and moved quickly to where the food was. A little old lady with a glass of milk and a muffin on her tray hurried to the empty space at the table and was about to put her tray down when the fat man's daughter said, "That place is taken."

Her voice almost scared me, and the way she talked, too. It sounded more like a man than a girl of nine or ten.

The little old lady said, "Oh, I'm sorry," and went away with the tray held out in front of her. She sounded like a little girl, and looked like one. Then a very swift-moving man with just a cup of coffee in his hand came to the table and again the fat man's daughter said, "That place is taken." But the man just sat down on the chair and began to sip his coffee quickly.

"It's not taken *now*," he said, "and I'll only be a minute."

The daughter looked at the mother, and they were both very angry at the man. I wondered why he didn't drink his coffee right where he had got it out of the spout, and then he brought a wrapped homemade sandwich out of his coat pocket, unwrapped it quickly, and began to eat it. He was all finished in a minute or two, and he got up and looked the fat man's daughter straight in the eye and said, "You see? No harm done at all." He looked at me then, and smiled, and then he did something that surprised me. He let his face stop being so excited and swift. He let it become very calm and quite serious, and then he said to me, "Thank you, my dear, for letting me share your table." I didn't know what to say, of course, but I just couldn't help smiling a little, and then he smiled, too, and went away quickly. Just in time, too, because the father was back with a new tray loaded with more stuff for them to eat. I thought it would be dessert, but it was three more orders of baked beans, but how did he know that that was what his wife and daughter wanted, too? He placed a plate in front of each of them, and without a word they all began to eat again. When they were finished I turned to Mama Girl to ask her to get ready to move to my table as soon as they got up, and Mama Girl didn't look very good. She looked very unhappy. She was reading something in the paper the man next to her was looking at.

"What is it?" I said.

"Oh, Frog," Mama Girl whispered. "John Dooley's dead. I just read it in the paper. He was one of the nicest directors in television I ever worked with, and I'm terribly unhappy. Everybody nice I meet dies, and I just can't understand it. He was fifty-one years old but he looked a lot younger and I never thought he would ever die."

Just then the three fat people at my table got up, and I said, "Come and sit at my table, Mama Girl."

Mama Girl picked up her tray and got up and began to move to my table, but just then three people, not even people together, took the three places at my table, and then somebody took the place Mama Girl had just left at the other table.

Mama Girl looked around for another place, but there just wasn't any.

"You stay right where you are," she said, "until I come back. Don't move, and be sure to eat every bit of your supper. All right? I'm very unhappy about poor John."

"All right."

Mama Girl went away and I finished my soup, and my ice cream, and then I began to drink my hot chocolate. At least once a week one of Mama Girl's friends dies, and it surprises her every time, and makes her very unhappy. Just thinking about it made me scared. Suppose we were to read in the paper some day that my father was dead in Paris? What then?

I drank my hot chocolate and felt very unhappy.

When I was all finished I looked around but I couldn't see Mama Girl anywhere. I just sat and waited, and then a woman with a tray came and said, "Are you finished, little girl?"

MAMA I LOVE YOU   67

"Yes, ma'am, but I've got to wait for my mother."

"Would you mind letting me sit down? You can stay right here, of course, until your mother comes back."

"All right," I said, and I got up, and the woman put her tray down on the table and sat down and began to eat. I looked around to see if I could find Mama Girl at one of the tables, but I couldn't. I wanted to go away from there and look for her, but I was afraid to, because then I might get lost, and I knew Mama Girl would be very upset about that, and then very angry, too, so I just kept standing and my feet began to get tired. I was about to go and look for Mama Girl anyway when I saw her at a table far away. I ran among the tables, but before I got to Mama Girl's table she got up and began to walk to the revolving door. I ran after her, but she got to the door before I did, and then she was out on Fifty-seventh Street, and I was still in the Automat. I ran through the people and bumped them and didn't care and didn't say excuse me or anything, and I got out to Fifty-seventh Street, too, and there was Mama Girl walking up toward Carnegie Hall.

"Mama Girl!" I screamed. She stopped suddenly, and turned around, but it wasn't Mama Girl, it was just somebody who looked a little like Mama Girl from far away but nothing like her from close up. I turned around and ran back to the revolving door and back into the Automat, and I was very scared. I ran back to where Mama Girl had asked me to wait, and I prayed to God to please let me find the table, and please let Mama Girl be there, and let us both go home to 2109 at the Pierre and get in bed and go to sleep. At first I didn't find the table, and then I did, because there was the woman who had asked if I was finished. Three new people were at the table with her now, and Mama Girl wasn't there. I went to the woman and I said, "Did my mother come here looking for me?"

"No, I don't believe so," the woman said.

"Can I stand here again?"

"Of course. Now, you just stop being frightened, and your mother will be here before you know it."

"Will she?"

"Of course."

Just then I saw Mama Girl making her way to the table, and I was so happy I hollered, "Mama Girl!" The woman looked up at me and smiled, and I thought she was just wonderful.

Mama Girl came and took my hand and we began to leave the Automat.

Chapter 11

A Loser in the Living Room, a Winner on TV

*I*t was wonderful just getting out of there, just getting away from the excitement and confusion of the people about eating. I don't think I understand eating. I know it's very important because I've been doing it all my life and most of the time I haven't even wanted to, and Mama Girl or Mother Viola or one or another of the other women who have come in by the day or to sleep in have asked me to please eat, or to please finish, or they have ordered me to, except Papa Boy—he never ordered me, he just laughed and said, "All right, Twink, eat—or else."

And then he lifted his right arm as if "or else" meant that he would bring it down on top of my head, but I always knew he never would and he knew I knew, and knew I liked to hear him say and see him do that. I always laughed, and most of the time I ate, too. My father didn't believe in ordering his kids to do anything.

One day he said, "I may be mistaken, but I'm opposed

to hitting a kid, except in self-defense." I wanted to know what self-defense was, and he said that if I were to lift a teaspoon and threaten him with it and he lifted me up, and threw me across the room, *that* would be self-defense, so I lifted the teaspoon, and he lifted me, and pretended to throw me across the room.

And then Mama Girl got mad at him, and they had another dinner-table fight while Pete and I watched.

We loved to watch them fight because all of a sudden each of them became somebody else, but at the same time stayed who they really are, and we never knew how long a fight would last. Sometimes it would go on all through dinner, but sometimes it would stop almost as soon as it had started, and then Pete and I would be disappointed.

One time Pete said, "Ah, Pop, that was no fight."

And Mama Girl got mad at Pete and told him to get up from the table immediately and go to his room and read *The World Book.*

Pete was glad to go, which only made Mama Girl madder than ever, and she said, "You see what happens? You go to work and throw your big personality all over the place, you practically crush every bone in the little girl's body, I stop you, we argue, and the kids *enjoy* it—they love to provoke us into a fight, and then when I try to punish them, they love *that,* too. I wish you'd take a course in how to be a father."

So then Papa Boy got mad, too, and they got into a real fight.

Pete sneaked back to the living room to hide behind the bookcase and watch and listen. But he got out of eating his supper, and he was always proud when he did that.

I just don't understand eating, that's all. I used to talk to Pete about it, and one day I said, "I wish children didn't have to eat at all, don't you? I wish we could live without eating—ever. All our lives from the beginning to the end."

Pete said, "You wish too much," so *we* had a fight, too.

When Mama Girl and I were finally out of the Automat and back on Fifty-seventh Street we looked at each other, and then Mama Girl bent down and hugged me, and there were tears in her eyes.

"I'm sorry your friend died, Mama Girl, but please don't feel bad."

"It's not that, Frog. I love you so much. Of course I'm sorry John Dooley's dead, too, but sometimes I forget how much I love you, and then I remember, and it makes me so glad tears come to my eyes."

"Oh, Mama Girl," I said. "You're my mother, you're my friend, you're my big sister, you're my little sister, you're the best, the prettiest, the nicest, you're everybody to me."

"Everybody but Papa Boy and Pete," she said, and that was true, and then she said, "Well, I'm sorry about that, Frog, I *really* am, but they're all right, I know they are, they always are, and it's not as if they're gone or anything like that, they're just in Paris, and we're *here*, that's all. They're probably walking in the streets somewhere right now."

We went to the curb in front of the Automat and then we turned around and looked in there at the little square-top tables, each with four little chairs, and the little cages with food in them, and the cafeteria part, and the people moving around and sitting and eating and getting up and going back for more or going out. We just stood there and watched it all, as if *we* were still in there.

"Never again," Mama Girl said.

"Well, maybe never again when it's so busy," I said.

"Not *that*, Frog."

"What, then?"

"Something else."

"What, Mama Girl?"

"I can't tell you."

"Sure you can."

"Well, never again—to make the mistakes I made."

"What mistakes?"

"To make them *on purpose*, too. To *insist* on making them. For what? For *this?* A divorced mother is silly."

"No, she's not, Mama Girl. She's beautiful."

"You're my girl, Frog."

We turned away from the Automat then, and went to the corner, and Mama Girl bought the *News* and the *Mirror* for tomorrow from the man in the stand there, and then we crossed Fifty-seventh, then Sixth Avenue, and began to walk toward Fifth Avenue.

It was nice there. It was very nice. The music stores with the pianos in the windows, and the stores with the little automobiles from Europe in them, and the art galleries with the paintings in them—we stopped and saw them all. It was nice because we were together, because we'd been out there at 1001 Macaroni Lane for a long time, but now we were in New York, and just yesterday we were back there and didn't know we would be in New York tomorrow.

There was a little crowd around the window of one store, so we stopped, too, and it was a television set with a big screen in the window of a music store. There was a nice man on the screen who spoke with an accent and his eyes were flashing because he was excited about something, but I didn't know what it was. With him was a young man, and he was nice, too. He was very friendly and sympathetic and he said to the man who spoke with an accent, "Well, Mr. Prato, last week you answered the sixteen-thousand dollar question correctly, and you've had all week to decide if you want to take the sixteen thousand dollars or try for thirty-two thousand. Have you made your decision?"

"Yes, I have," the man said. "I went to church and prayed to God to tell me what to do, and with God's help I want to go on."

The young man got excited and everybody who was in the place applauded and cheered and whispered. The young man turned to a man at a desk with two policemen standing beside him, and the man at the desk reached into a safe and brought out an envelope and handed it to the young man. He took the man who spoke with an accent to a soundproof booth that looked something like a telephone booth, and the man who wanted to go on went in there. He looked alone in there, and scared, and everybody who was in that place became quiet. The man in the booth crossed himself, and then the young man opened the envelope and brought out a piece of paper, and he said, "All right, now, Dino, don't be frightened. I'll read the question straight through once, and then you will have thirty seconds to make your answer—for thirty-two thousand dollars." The young man looked at the slip of paper with the question on it, and then he said, "Dino, the question is in four parts." Then he read the question, and I didn't think anybody in the whole world would be able to answer one part, let alone all four parts, and it didn't look as if the man in the booth would even be able to *remember* the four parts. An orchestra played scary music for thirty seconds while the poor man tried to think of the question and the four correct answers, and then the music stopped, and it was very exciting.

"Will he know the answers, Mama Girl?"

"How *could* he?"

The man who spoke with an accent said, "The opera is *Aïda.* The place where Arturo Toscanini conducted it was Brazil. It was first performed in Cairo, Egypt. It was Christmas Eve."

"Right!" the young man hollered, and then everybody screamed, and everybody in the street was happy. The man came out of the booth and shook hands with the young man. It looked as if there were tears in his eyes when he waved to the people who were cheering him, and then he threw a kiss to somebody. I guess it was his wife and kids at home, and now he'd done it, he'd answered every part of the question correctly, and he had won thirty-two thousand dollars. The young man was very happy for him and told him to go home for a week and think about whether he would take the thirty-two thousand dollars or go on and try for sixty-four thousand dollars.

We went walking on down Fifty-seventh Street to Fifth Avenue, and we both felt happy about the man, as if we knew him, and his family, and were proud that he knew so much about opera.

"I hope he doesn't try for sixty-four thousand," Mama Girl said. "They'll ask him a question with sixty-four thousand parts."

"No, they won't," I said. "And next week he can bring the greatest authority in the world on opera with him— the man *said* so. I just can't wait to find out if he'll take the money, or try for more."

"Neither can I," Mama Girl said. "It's certainly something to live for."

We walked up Fifth Avenue, looking into the store windows, and came to the Pierre. We went in and got our key and got in an elevator and went up to twenty-one, down the hall, to the right, and there we were at home, good old 2109.

We went in and took off our clothes and jumped in bed, and Mama Girl hugged me, and we talked and laughed, and then I don't remember any more, because I was asleep, and happy.

Chapter 12

Strawberries and Cream, Lamb Chops and Watercress

*I*n the morning the telephone rang, but Mama Girl didn't jump up and answer it, so I put my mouth close to her ear and said, "The telephone, Mama Girl."

Without opening her eyes Mama Girl said, "Please answer it for me. Tell them I'm asleep. Tell them to call me tomorrow."

I jumped out of bed and answered the phone. It was Mike McClatchey, only he thought I was Mama Girl.

"Get your little daughter and let's have breakfast," he said. "I'm downstairs."

"Mr. McClatchey," I said, "my mother's asleep, and she says please call her tomorrow."

"Mr. McClatchey?" Mama Girl said. She jumped out of bed and took the receiver out of my hand and talked quickly and laughed and said we'd be right down—just give us fifteen minutes.

She hung up, and then there was a lot of running

around in 2109. Mama Girl drew a bath while we both brushed our teeth, then we both got in and soaped and rinsed, then we both got out and dried, then we got dressed in our best matching dresses: bright yellow with little white flowers all over.

When we ran out of the room to the elevator Miss Cranshaw was there, and she said, "Well, there you are, aren't you?"

"Yes," I said, and then she said, "I was afraid I might not see you again. Will you have tea with me again soon?"

"Yes. This is my mother."

Miss Cranshaw smiled at Mama Girl and said, "I'm learning so much from your daughter. I do hope you can come this afternoon—anytime after five."

Mama Girl smiled and said, "All right."

The elevator came and we got in, but it was morning and the whole elevator was packed. I got between Mama Girl and Miss Cranshaw, and they kept me from being squashed. When we got out of the elevator I saw a very distinguished-looking man with a very thin mustache. He was holding two bouquets of violets. Miss Cranshaw stepped out first. She went to the man and took both bouquets and kissed him and said, "Why, Mike McClatchey, how sweet of you."

Mike McClatchey said, "Kate, you know I've *always* adored you."

Mama Girl and I got out of the way of the people, and we stood together near Mike McClatchey and Kate Cranshaw.

"If you adored me," Miss Cranshaw said, "you wouldn't have brought me violets. You would have remembered that my favorite flower is the red blossom of the prickly cactus."

She turned to Mama Girl and me, and she handed each of us a bouquet of violets.

"After five, then," she said.

"Do you know one another?" Mike McClatchey said.

"Oh, my goodness, yes of course," Kate Cranshaw said. "You know perfectly well that I know everybody who has talent. And these two are just loaded with talent."

"Thanks to *you*, I suppose," Mike McClatchey said.

"Not at all," Miss Cranshaw said. "As a matter of fact, I'm taking lessons from *her*," and she put her hand on my head. "Have a pleasant day, then, all of you."

"Let's have a long talk real soon," Mike McClatchey said. "I need some help on this new play."

"I'll call you," Miss Cranshaw said.

"You said that the last time we met, almost a year ago. Let *me* call you."

"Don't you dare. This time I *will* call you."

"When?"

"Will tomorrow morning be soon enough?"

"I'll be waiting, Kate."

Miss Cranshaw spoke to Mama Girl now. "Bring the play to tea, will you?"

Mama Girl looked at Mike McClatchey, and then she said, "All right."

Miss Cranshaw walked down the long hall. She walked as if she were a queen.

"What luck," Mike McClatchey said. "I had no idea you knew Kate Cranshaw. If I can get her to help me with my people in this play, I'll feel a lot easier about its chances."

"I *don't* know her," Mama Girl said. "My daughter does."

"I might have known," Mike said.

Mama Girl introduced me to Mr. McClatchey, then we went into a big room full of light. We sat at a table with a thick white tablecloth on it, and we had breakfast together.

"It's my favorite meal of the day," Mike McClatchey said, "and I hope it's yours, too. •I really can't enjoy breakfast unless everybody else does, and I've got to have a big one, too."

We started with strawberries and cream, and then the waiter brought a silver dish with scrambled eggs and crisp bacon in it, and another with broiled lamb chops in it, with fresh watercress, and another with home-fried potatoes in it.

Mike McClatchey served Mama Girl and me first, and then he served himself, and he began to eat, and so did Mama Girl, and then so did I. We just ate and ate, and talked and joked and laughed, and he was one of the nicest men I ever saw. He wasn't a young man, he was fifty five, he said so himself, but he was tall and very strong, and his eyes were very young. His face was long and narrow, and very serious when he wasn't telling a joke or laughing, only he almost always was. His hair was thick and gray and parted in a very straight line on the left side. After we had had breakfast he brought a flat brown envelope out of his brief case and handed it to Mama Girl.

"There it is," he said. "Please read it as soon as you can. Aloud, I mean, so Twink will know what it's all about. It *is* Twink, isn't it?"

"It's her father's name for her."

"It suits her."

"She's got eight or nine others."

"All right," Mike McClatchey said. "Read it, and take it to Kate when you go to tea. She'll probably ask you both to read. Pay a lot of attention to everything she says. She's the greatest. She can teach you more in ten minutes than you might learn in ten years."

"Mike," Mama Girl said, "I'm absolutely thrilled, but I

flew here from California to go to work in the theater, not to put my daughter to work."

"Give me time, will you?" Mike said.

"Well, *is* there a part for me, or not?"

"At this moment, no, but if everything else goes well, we'll see what we can do."

"But you *do* want Twink?"

"Yes, and how *is* her father?"

"He's quite well," Mama Girl said, "but you haven't heard her read."

"I've heard her speak and I've *seen* her," Mike said.

"Are you *sure* you want her?"

"Yes. It's up to her now—and you."

"Well, then," Mama Girl said, "speak to her."

"No," Mike said.

"Why not?"

"If she were *my* daughter, I wouldn't let her do it," Mike said. "I love the theater. I even love actors, and you know they're not easy to love, but I couldn't take the responsibility of urging this girl to come into the theater."

"I don't want to take that responsibility, either," Mama Girl said. "After all, she isn't my daughter alone. She's also her father's, and he knows nothing about this."

"That's what I mean," Mike said. "Just read the play aloud, as if it were a game. You and Twink talk about it. Find out how she really feels. And then if the next step is to let her father know, phone him."

"He's in Paris."

"They've got phones in Paris."

"I'm thrilled, Mike. I really am. Because I know you want her, but I'm terribly let down about me."

"Now, don't be," Mike said. "One thing at a time. I've got a few ideas."

"Like what?"

"Well, for one thing the three of us could have breakfast or lunch tomorrow with the playwright. After all, he's the boss, but I believe he'll soon get the same idea I got when I saw you together."

"What idea?"

"His might even be a little better than mine. I'm just a producer. Let's wait. Now, go on out and have a walk in the Park. You look a lot fresher this morning than you did yesterday at lunch."

"I was sick," Mama Girl said. "We both were. We had fevers. An airplane ride does that to us. Now I'm just sleepy."

"Well, have a nice nap after your walk, then read the play, then go along to Kate's for tea. I'll be waiting to hear from you. If I'm not at my office, phone me at home."

"I'm absolutely thrilled, Mike."

"How about you, Twink?" Mike said.

"I'm thrilled, too."

"Are you, really?"

"Yes. I love to walk in the Park."

Mike McClatchey and Mama Girl laughed, so I laughed, too, but I *do* love to walk in the Park.

We got up and walked together to Fifth Avenue. Mike jumped into a taxi, and Mama Girl and I crossed Fifth Avenue to the Park, to go in and walk there.

Chapter 13

All About a Little Girl

We had a nice walk in the Park, and then went back to the Pierre and up to 2109.

Mama Girl opened the flat brown envelope and brought out the play.

"Is *that* a play?"

"Yes, but it's in manuscript. It hasn't been performed yet. It may not even be finished yet. The playwright may want to add something to it, or change something, or take something out."

"What's the name of it?"

"*A Bouncing Ball*—by Emerson Tully."

"Emerson Tully?"

"Yes, he's the man who wrote it, of course."

"Do you know him?"

"No, I don't."

"Have you heard of him?"

"No, I haven't. I guess he's a new playwright. Almost all of the new ones like to send their plays to Mike McClatchey because he's not afraid to produce new plays by new playwrights, and he goes to a lot of trouble to do a good job every time."

Mama Girl turned a page and then she said, "Well, are you ready, Frog?"

"Are you going to read it?"

"Yes."

"*All* of it?"

"Every word of it. You just make yourself comfortable. Lie down if you like and just listen."

"But I thought you were going to take a nap first."

"No, I'm wide-awake now. I'm much too excited to be able to take a nap. All right?"

"All right, but how long will it take?"

"Oh, to do it right, I suppose it'll take two hours, but it may take even longer."

"Do we *have* to read all of it?"

"Of course, Frog."

"Why?"

"Oh, now, don't you go stupid on me all of a sudden, young lady, because I'm fighting for my life."

"I have a right to ask why we have to read all of it, don't I?"

"No, you don't!"

Mama Girl hollered at me, and there it was again—another fight. We just have to have at least one every day.

Mama Girl threw the play against the wall and said, "I don't want it. I don't want any part of it. It's too humiliating. If I can't get a part on my own appearance and ability, then I don't want any part at all. If I've got to tag along into the theater with my daughter, the hell with the theater."

She began to cry, and then she hollered at me, "I hate you!"

So I hollered at her, "Then I hate you, too!"

And I began to cry a little, too. Only I'm ashamed to cry. I always have been. I guess it's because my brother Peter Bolivia Agriculture was always ashamed to, too.

He said, "Crying's for grown-ups, not for us. They cry all the time."

While she was crying, Mama Girl picked up the play and began to smooth out the pages that had got smashed.

I don't like to see her unhappy, so I said, "I'm sorry. I want to hear the play. Every word of it."

"No," Mama Girl said. "You're just saying that because you're so superior. I'll phone Mike McClatchey at his office and tell him to take his play and stick it up."

"No, please don't do that."

"I'm ashamed of myself," Mama Girl said, "and I don't enjoy that. I'll try other producers. If I fail, O.K., so what have I lost? We'll fly back to California and just live, that's all. Just look at television and read newspapers, and forget all about the theater."

But she didn't go to the telephone. I couldn't tell her I liked being in New York, but also liked being in my own home in California. I liked my whole neighborhood, and all my friends whose mothers and fathers *weren't* divorced, whose fathers *weren't* in Paris, whose mothers *didn't* want to go on the stage, who just lived in their houses.

I couldn't tell her anything because we had come all the way to New York so she could try once more.

Little by little her voice changed. It stopped being angry and excited and unhappy. It became clear and serious, and she began to read the play.

"This play happens to a little girl," she read. "The little girl is eight or nine, or ten or eleven, and she has many friends, most of them imaginary. She is very earnest, but she is not an unhappy little girl. There is nothing the matter with her at all. She just imagines things, including real things. Things that really happen to her are no different from things she imagines. She is very real, and everything she imagines is very real."

Mama Girl stopped reading to light a Parliament, and then she looked at me. She didn't say anything. She just waited. I knew she expected me to say something, so I said, "I like it."

"Do you really, Frog? Because if you do—well, at least I can *read* it to you, and then—"

"It'll be time to go to tea at Miss Cranshaw's."

"You *like* her, don't you?"

"Oh, yes. Don't you?"

"I do, of course, but she's so intelligent and famous, I'm a little afraid of her."

"Oh, that's silly, Mama Girl."

"No, it's not," Mama Girl said. "I'm afraid she'll see through me, and I'm *nothing.*"

"Now, you cut that out, Mama Girl. You know you don't believe that."

"It's the truth. I just want to be famous and rich, I don't want to study hard and work hard. I just want everything brought to me on a silver platter. She'll see straight through me, because I want so much—but you, you just don't want anything, so of course she's *got* to love you."

"Oh, Mama Girl, will you please read the play and stop fighting? I *said* I'm sorry, didn't I?"

"Why should you be sorry?" Mama Girl said. "You haven't done anything wrong. I have. And I *am* sorry, Frog. Really, I am. I get ugly because I'm so angry about my silly life. All I want is more for me—ME. I want to be the most beautiful girl of all, I want to be the most famous, I want to be rich—and it makes me ugly."

"No, it doesn't, Mama Girl. You're *beautiful* when you're ugly. I mean, you're *always* beautiful, no matter how you feel, or what you do."

"I'm not," Mama Girl said, but just then the telephone rang, and it was Gladys Dubarry. Mama Girl spoke to her quickly, and not very politely, either, and then she said good-by and hung up.

She got the hotel operator and said, "Please don't ring here until further notice. I'm working."

She read the whole play from beginning to end. It was funny sometimes, and sometimes sad. Once or twice it was something else, too, only I don't know what, but it made me feel all excited inside, and a little scared, too.

It was all about a little girl and the things she imagined, and the things that really happened to her.

There were tears in Mama Girl's eyes when she came to the end. She didn't say anything for a long time, and then she said very softly, "I know that little girl, because I *was* that little girl. I *still* am. Do you like the play, Frog?"

"Yes, Mama Girl."

"I'm glad, but I want to take a nap now. I want to go to sleep and remember the whole play all over again—my whole life."

"I want to, too."

We stretched out on top of the bed, and after a few minutes Mama Girl was fast asleep. I thought about the play, and about Mama Girl, and what she had just said, and then I looked at her, and it was true, she *was* the little girl in the play, she was *still* the little girl, only now she was thirty-three years old, and she had a daughter of her own who was nine years old—me.

I remembered the things the little girl had imagined, and I imagined a few of my own. They mixed together, and I didn't know for sure which was which.

I cuddled up to Mama Girl, I put my arms around her, and I went to sleep.

Chapter 14

The Lions and Tigers on the Front Lawn

I dreamed a dream that scared me, because there was so much danger in it.

I was back in Pacific Palisades. Deborah Schlomb came to the window of my room and tapped on the glass, but even before I went to look I knew it was my best pal Deb. I went to the window and Deb didn't say anything, but I knew she wanted me to go out there right away. I thought it was night, and then I noticed that it wasn't. How could it be night when the whole front lawn was crowded with birds of all kinds?—very little birds, like hummers, medium-sized birds, like sparrows, mockers, and blackbirds, and big birds, like hawks. How could it be night when the sun was making orange light through the eucalyptus trees at the edge of the garden, and then ten or eleven other suns were shining and making ten or eleven other colors of light? Deb was dressed in ballet clothes, so I knew something special was going on. I ran to the closet to get my ballet clothes that I wore when I took dancing lessons. I put them on and ran to see if Mama Girl was still asleep, and she was. She was fast asleep, but so was Papa Boy, and what was *he* doing there? He was supposed to be in Paris, wasn't he? So then I ran to Peter Bolivia Agriculture's room, and there he was in his bed, fast asleep, too—but the minute I reached his bed, to make sure it *was* him, he opened his eyes.

"Hello, Frog," he said. He was the one who gave me that name when I was very little.

"Hello, Pete. When did you and Papa Boy get back?"

"What are you talking about? Get back from *where?*"

"Paris, of course."

"Ah, you're dreaming," Pete said.

"No, I'm not, Pete. Are you going to stay?"

"Ah, go to sleep, will you? It's night."

"If you think it's night, look out the window."

Pete jumped out of bed and ran to the window. He took one look and said, "Holy cow. What are all those people doing on the front lawn?"

"You mean birds, don't you?" I looked again, and now there wasn't one bird out there. Just people of all kinds. They were just standing there. And it *was* night. I looked for Deb, but she wasn't there.

"Go back to sleep," Pete said, so I did, but the minute I was asleep again I heard tapping at the window again, so I jumped out of bed and ran to the window, and there was Deb again, and the whole front lawn was covered with lions and tigers, but Deb wasn't afraid of them at all, and neither was I. She wanted me to get out there with her, so I ran to the closet again, and this time I put on my favorite play dress, but I hadn't forgotten that Papa Boy was home again, so I ran to have another look at him, but he wasn't there anymore, it was just Mama Girl, and she looked all alone. I ran to Peter Bolivia Agriculture's room, but he wasn't there anymore, either. I ran out of the house and there was Deb, but not one lion or tiger out there, and not one bird, either.

"What happened to everybody?" I said.

"My mother says I can walk up the hill to the village and spend ten cents," Deb said. "Does your mother say you can, too?"

"She's asleep," I said, "and I haven't got ten cents, but I'll walk with you, anyhow."

We walked up the hill to the village and all around Woolworth's looking at things, and then Deb spent her ten cents. She bought a green ribbon for a nickel, and a red one for another, and she asked me to please tie one of the ribbons into her hair.

"Which one?"

"Oh, either one," she said, so I tied the red one, and then she tied the green one in my hair, and I said, "Oh, thank you, Deb, but I'll give it back when we get home."

We walked back down the hill to our neighborhood, and everybody noticed our new ribbons. We talked and laughed the whole time, and then she said it was time for her to go home, so I said, "All right, Deb, and thanks for letting me go to the village with you, and for tying the ribbon in my hair. You can have it back now."

"Oh, no," Deb said. "It's yours for keeps."

"Then I'll buy one for *you* and tie it in your hair just as soon as I get the money."

"So long," Deb said.

"So long," I said.

She went home, and I went inside to see what was going on at 1001 Macaroni Lane.

Mama Girl was sitting on her bed, talking to Clara Coolbaw on the telephone.

"Frog," she said, "be a good girl and start a pot of coffee, will you, and when it's ready bring me a cup."

"O.K.," I said.

That was the dream, and the part that scared me wasn't the lions and tigers, it was when my father wasn't there anymore.

Now I was awake and Mama Girl was sitting on the edge of the bed in 2109 at the Pierre in New York talking long-distance to Clara Coolbaw in California.

"It's the most beautiful play I've ever read," she said.

Clara Coolbaw must have said something funny, because Mama Girl howled, and hollered, "Oh, you mean thing, you."

They talked and talked, as if it didn't cost anything, and then at last they said good-by, and Mama Girl hung up. When she saw me she said, "How long have you been awake?"

"Six or seven minutes, I guess."

"I phoned her to tell her to go out to the house and look after the goldfish. I told her all about the play, too."

"Mama Girl," I said, "what does it mean when you dream you're home and your father's there, and your brother, too?"

"It means you'd like to be home, and you'd like them to be there, too."

"I know it means *that*, but what *else* does it mean?"

"I don't know," Mama Girl said. "The dream's made you unhappy, hasn't it?"

"A little, I guess."

"Well, don't be. Be happy and twinkle. Be happy and dance every minute you're awake, the way you always do."

"I get tired of being happy sometimes. After all, I'm nine years old, I'm not a child."

Mama Girl stretched out on the bed and took me in her arms and hugged me and said, "Nobody is ever a child, Frog, and nobody ever stops being one. That's how it is."

"Why is it that way?"

"Because fathers and mothers were never children, either. And they never stopped being children, either. It goes on and on that way. It's the way it is, and all we can do is our best."

She looked at her wristwatch and then she said, "Well, it's a little after five. Shall we go to tea?"

"Do you want to go?"

"Oh, yes. Do you?"

"I guess so—if you do."

"But I thought you *liked* Miss Cranshaw."

"I do, but that doesn't mean I want to go to tea."

"Oh, what's the matter, Frog?"

"In my dream I talked to my brother, but I didn't talk to my father. I didn't know it was a dream. I didn't want to wake him up. I thought I'd talk to him later on. Now it's too late."

"What did you want to say to him?"

"Nothing. I just wanted to talk to him. What does a little girl *ever* say to her father? She just likes to see him, that's all. She just likes to hear him and know he's there. She just likes to smell him. She doesn't like *girls and women* all the time."

"Oh, you *are* in a bad mood, aren't you?"

"I'm just sorry I didn't talk to my father."

"Well, call him in Paris."

"Oh, that's not the same at all. He was home. We all were. Besides, we can't afford it."

"Well, call him collect."

"Oh, Mama Girl, I wouldn't do a thing like that. I'll wait until I dream about him again, and next time I'll remember to speak to him."

"How was he?"

"He looked fine, but of course he was asleep."

"Where?"

"In bed, of course."

"What bed?"

"His bed, and your bed, at home in California. The bed that you sleep alone in now."

"Oh. Where was I?"

"You were in bed, too."

"How was *I*?"

"You were fine. You looked better than I've seen you in a long time."

"Why? Have I been looking as bad as all that?"

"No, but you looked better when my father was home."

"Your father," Mama Girl said. "Well, don't forget I'm your mother. Just because we're together all the time doesn't mean I'm not somebody important, too. Now, I've been thinking about the play. I've been thinking about it over and over."

"I know, because it's all about you."

"Well, it is, but I've been thinking about the play not because it's about me, but because Mike McClatchey wants *you* to play the part of the little girl, and I don't know what you want to do, or even if you can *ever* decide for yourself what you want to do, and then if you happen to decide that you want to try to do the part, I don't know if I should let you. I don't know if your father would want you to become a child actress. I'm troubled about the whole thing, and if we're going to have tea with Miss Cranshaw, it's about time we got going. If we're not going, then it's about time we let her know. What do you want to do, Frog? *Really?* I have got to try my best not to force you to decide to do something you really don't want to do. If we go to tea, Miss Cranshaw will expect us to take the play, and then most likely she will ask you to read, and I know that when you do she is going to be very

excited and she is going to want to help you, if you need
help, and she thinks you don't, and she is going to want
you to take the part. And that means a whole change in
your life, and in mine, too. So what do you think?"

"I think we have got to go to tea, because we said we
would."

"Do you think you will be able to make up your mind for
yourself about doing the part for Mike McClatchey?"

"I don't know. It must be very hard work to be a little
girl you aren't—every evening on a stage in front of
people."

"Yes, it *is* very hard work, but it's not hard to be a little
girl you aren't—that part's easy. The part that's hard is
learning *how* to be that little girl, or to make that little
girl be who *you* are. Do you think you might want to try,
because if you don't, I'll understand, and we'd better not
go to tea. We'd better just tell Mike McClatchey you don't
want to be a child actress."

"Will they pay me money?"

"Of course they will. You're practically the whole play.
They'll pay you a lot."

"Can I spend some of the money?"

"Of course you can. It's your money. Every penny you
earn will be yours, not mine. It'll be put in a trust for you.
You'll probably be rich at the age of ten."

"All right, then," I said, "let's go to tea."

"You've decided you want to do the part, then?" Mama
Girl said.

"I've decided I want to go to tea, because I want to
know what Miss Cranshaw thinks I ought to do. I've
never thought about a thing like this before. I don't know
if I can be a special kind of little girl on purpose, but I
want to go to tea."

"I think that that's quite reasonable and intelligent,"

Mama Girl said, "but before we go, will you please stop being so grown-up and sad. I just can't help feeling useless and unkind when you're so much more intelligent and orderly than I am. So will you please think about happy things a moment?"

"All right, Mama Girl."

I jumped off the bed and began to dance, because that's what I always do when I feel good, or want to stop feeling bad, but of course Mama Girl has never known that I've danced most of the time to stop feeling bad, she thinks I've always danced because I've felt wonderful, but I haven't. That's why her best friend Clara Coolbaw calls me Mrs. Nijinsky.

"This girl has *got* to be the prima ballerina of Nicaragua," Clara Coolbaw said to Mama Girl a long time ago. "She's dancing all the time."

But a lot she knows about anything. A lot she knows about little girls, even though she's got two of her own. I'll bet she doesn't know the first thing about either of her girls. She just likes to hold her nose high and talk swift and silly.

Chapter 15

A Quiet Chat
with Dr. Sprang

*W*e were getting ready to go to tea when somebody knocked at our door. It was my doctor, A. J. Sprang.

I said, "Thank you very much for the doll."

He said, "Well, now, the *both* of you look like dolls—Mama Doll and Daughter Doll. How do you *feel?*"

"I'm afraid we've been quarrelsome the whole day," Mama Girl said.

"Really? Why?"

"A divorced mother is always on the defensive, even with her own daughter, I suppose."

"Why not pretend you're *not* divorced, then?"

"But I *am.*"

"Of course, but how *divorced* can you be? You're still her mother, and her father is still her father. Every time a husband and a wife are divorced the world doesn't stop."

The little doctor put both his hands under my chin and felt in there and he said, *"Does* it?"

"No," I said, "the world doesn't *ever* stop."

"Of course not. Have you both been eating and resting well?"

"That's just about all we *have* been doing," Mama Girl said. "And I'm a little fed up with it, too."

"Oh, not at all," the little doctor said. "Just choose nicer things to eat, and nicer ways to rest. Now, melons, for instance. This time of year melons are wonderful."

"We had strawberries at breakfast," I said.

"And did you enjoy them?"

"Very much."

"And what did you have for lunch?"

"We skipped lunch because we'd had such a big breakfast, and now we're going to tea."

"Tea," the little doctor said. "What fun tea can be—for the right people."

He looked at Mama Girl and then he said, "How long have you been divorced, my dear?"

"Three years," Mama Girl said, "but the first two years my husband—well, my *ex*-husband—stayed quite close to us. Almost a year now, though, he's been far away, and my son has been with him. That means that this girl hasn't had a father and a brother for a year, except in her memory, and she *does* remember them—quite a lot, I may say. It puts me on the defensive, and so she and I fight a lot."

"Yes, that *does* happen, doesn't it? They're well, are they? Both of them?"

"Well, they've never written that they weren't, so I suppose they are, but, then, who knows? Their letters from Paris are full of fun, though. I'm sure they must be well."

"Paris? And what are they doing there?"

"My husband is a composer. He just thought he'd like to go to Paris and live there for a while."

"A composer? Now, there *is* a profession, but can a man earn a living as a composer?"

"My *husband* always has. He works very hard all the time, but he loves his work, and he insists on making money, too. He doesn't believe art should be some sort of delicate flower in a world of money and machines. My husband has a very strong personality and he quarrels with everybody he has ever met. I once heard him brag that he had never kept a friend. He prefers enemies."

"Wonderful," the little doctor said.

"I'm one of his enemies," Mama Girl said.

"No, you're not," I said. "You *know* you're not. My father has all kinds of people he knows and likes, but he's just too busy to have friends. But he doesn't really have *one* enemy in the whole world, either. He's just as busy not having enemies as he is not having friends."

"Well," Mama Girl said to the doctor, "that's what I mean. We have a little quarrel going all the time, but every once in a while it gets to be big, and then I'm really on the defensive, because I know she understands him better than I do."

"Ah, well," the doctor said, "you're a nice family. The man and boy in Paris, the woman and girl in New York. Now, it could be a lot worse, couldn't it?"

"That's always true," Mama Girl said. "Almost every day somebody I know dies, and to me nothing is worse than that. Just last night in the Automat I read in a neighbor's paper that John Dooley had died. There's no telling who'll be next."

"Yes, that's true. I have more friends dead than I have alive."

"But they *are* friends."

"Oh, I just *call* them friends. They're people I met and knew a little, but not very much. I *do* miss them, though."

The little doctor smiled and went to the door. He hadn't sat down the whole time, not even for a minute.

"Well," he said, "you're both in perfect health, but if you're going to be here for a while I hope you won't mind if I drop by from time to time. I frequently visit Miss Cranshaw down the hall."

"That's where we're having tea," I said.

"Oh, is it?"

"Yes."

"Well, she doesn't often have people to visit her, and I've heard many people would *like* to, especially people in the theater, so I think you're entitled to feel pleased."

"We *are* pleased."

"Good-by, then," the little doctor said, and he went.

Mama Girl looked at me and she said, "Now, Frog, please try to understand that all I want is for you to have fun—right now at Miss Cranshaw's, and then every day until you're a big girl and fall in love and get married. I don't want you to go on the stage, but at the same time I don't want to stop you if that's what you want to do."

"Oh, I understand, Mama Girl. Don't worry about me. I have fun. I always have fun."

"You do, don't you?" Mama Girl said. "If I didn't believe you did, I think I would die of shame."

We went out of 2109 and began to walk down the hall to the door of Miss Cranshaw's apartment.

Chapter 16

Man, What You Doing in Paris, Boy?

At first Kate Cranshaw was the same with Mama Girl and me as she had been with me alone—we all talked and listened and joked and laughed and drank tea and ate cookies and cakes and very thin triangles of white bread covered with various nice-tasting spreads, and then Miss Cranshaw said to Mama Girl, "As luck would have it, Mike McClatchey left a copy of the play at the desk, so that when I got back early this afternoon I decided to read it, something I rarely do, I may say. I mean, I'm sent so many plays, and so many of them just aren't worth reading, that's all. I'm devoted to the theater, as you know, but for many years I've been angry about the kind of plays our playwrights have been writing. When the plays have been effective, they've been about sick, hysterical people—and, I'm sorry, they bore me. That's the price one must pay, I suppose, for not being an amateur, for being a professional, for knowing better."

Miss Cranshaw picked up a copy of the play off her desk and said, "This is one of the most poorly constructed plays I've ever read, but at the same time it's one of the most beautiful and simple and—well, *straight*. And I prefer straight things. Have you read it?"

"Yes," Mama Girl said.

"Aloud?"

"Yes."

Miss Cranshaw looked at me. "Then, of course, you *heard* your mother read it."

"Yes."

Now Miss Cranshaw walked around in the big room. I guess she was thinking. Every now and then she stopped and looked first at me and then at Mama Girl, but we didn't say anything.

"Let me tell you what I think," she said at last. "I think Mike will give this play a magnificent production. He will spare no expense. The play will come alive, as it should. It will please and satisfy *me* very deeply. And it will fail."

Miss Cranshaw said the word *fail* in a way that made me want to burst into tears, but of course I didn't. I just looked away until I didn't want to burst any more. She said the word as if it hurt her to say it. *Fail.* If something beautiful fails—something simple and straight—then *everything* fails, and everybody is hurt—that is the way she said it.

"I called Mike on the telephone an hour ago," she said. "I told him what I've just told you. I said I had no right *not* to tell him what I believe. I asked him if he was still going to produce the play. He didn't hesitate an instant in saying that he was. I admire him for that, but I feel sorry for him, too. Mike is a pro. He could produce hits if he wanted to. It isn't anywhere near as difficult to do as people imagine. It's a matter of choice, pure and simple. If you choose a safe play, and produce it effectively, you have a hit. Right now Mike *needs* a hit. He hasn't had one in three seasons. One more failure and he may be in serious trouble. Even so, this play *should* be produced."

Miss Cranshaw spoke very clearly, as if somebody else were listening.

"But it *will* fail. The best critics will like it, the others won't, and the people who buy tickets to plays won't— they just won't, that's all. I'm almost seventy years old. I've been in the theater since I was a little girl. Even now, I will take a part if I like it, but for more than twenty years I've tried to teach others how to act—or, to put it another way, how to be people, which does not happen by itself. It happens on purpose. Any of us is something because we choose to be something. I am speaking on the level of art, of course. Everybody is *something or other*, of course, but on the level of art nobody is anything accidentally."

Miss Cranshaw stopped suddenly. She went to the window and stood there, looking out. I looked at Mama Girl. She looked very happy, and I couldn't understand why, because everything Miss Cranshaw had said was so unhappy. After a minute Miss Cranshaw came and poured tea into our cups again, and she said very cheerfully, "I love to stand at that window and look down at the people in the Park. What a stage-setting the Park is, and what a wonderful play goes on there every day. Children and their mothers and fathers. Strangers and little dogs. Birds and squirrels, and then at the Zoo all kinds of animals in *cages.*"

We sipped tea and waited. I knew we were waiting, because Mama Girl wasn't saying anything. So I waited, too. If Mama Girl hadn't been there, I know I wouldn't have waited. I would have talked, too. At last it happened.

Miss Cranshaw looked at Mama Girl and said, "Do you want your daughter to play the part of the little girl in the play?"

"Do *you* want her to?" Mama Girl said.

"Now, that isn't fair," Miss Cranshaw said. "Answer *my* question, and then I'll answer yours."

"Then, the answer is no," Mama Girl said. "I don't want her to appear in a play, because I don't think her father would want her to."

"Not *a play,*" Miss Cranshaw said. "*This* play. And it's not the same thing at all."

"Well, not even in *this* play," Mama Girl said. "I don't want her to appear in it, because she would have to work very hard, and I don't believe I have a right to expect her to. At the same time, if *she* decides she *wants* to appear in it, I will do everything I can to keep her well and happy."

"Why do you feel her father would be against it?"

"He loves her. He wants her to be a little girl, and nothing more—his daughter. He's written to her once a week for a whole year. Not to me, but to her. He works hard to provide for her—and for me—and he doesn't want her to have a care in the world. Of course, she *has* cares just the same, but is there a child who doesn't?"

"If he were to read the play, might he change his mind?"

"I don't know, but I'm sure he'd like the play. I'm sure he'd *see* his daughter as the little girl, and then I think he'd say no, nothing doing, leave her alone."

"Would he be likely to ask her to decide for herself?"

"Absolutely not. I'm sure of *that.* It isn't that he doesn't respect the wishes of his children. He does. But he's suspicious of any wish that isn't entirely for fun."

"Suppose his daughter wanted to be in the play—for fun?"

"He wouldn't believe she's able to decide for herself."

"Has he a legal right to stop her from appearing in the play?"

"Of course not. Neither of us has any *particular* legal

rights. We're divorced, that's all, but we haven't stopped being parents to our children. If he didn't want her to be in the play, I would *have* to ask her not to be in it."

"Even if she were sure she wanted to be in it?"

"Yes."

Miss Cranshaw smiled, and then she looked at me.

"All right, now, Twink," she said. "Yesterday when you and I had tea we talked the whole time and had a lot of fun. But not today. So far you've done very little talking, but now it's your turn. Do you like the little girl in the play?"

"Yes," I said.

"Oh, now," Miss Cranshaw said. "Don't stop. This is not a trial. It's tea, and fun."

"Well," I said, "I don't know what to talk *about.*"

"The little girl, of course."

"Well, I like her, but I don't *know* her."

"Do you like the things she imagines, and the things that happen to her?"

"Yes."

"Would you like to perform the part of the little girl in the play?"

"I would, but I can't."

"Because your father might not want you to?"

"No, because I can't *be* another little girl. I can only be me."

"Could you *pretend* to be another little girl?"

"Of course. I do all the time, but not just little girls. I pretend to be my mother, too. I also pretend to be pitchers.

"Pitchers?"

"In baseball, because when I grow up I'm going to pitch for the New York Giants."

"Why are you going to pitch for *them?*"

"Because my brother's going to pitch for the Brooklyn Dodgers."

"I see."

"I pretend to be animals, too. I pretend to be everybody. And everything, too."

"Such as?"

"Well, if I see a bright star, I pretend to be a star."

"How?"

"I pretend to be right here but far away, too, and I pretend I'm shining just like the star."

"Is that why your father calls you Twink?"

"No. I never told him I pretend to be a star. He just started calling me Twink one day, that's all."

"All right," Miss Cranshaw said. "Why does your mother call you Frog?"

"I love 'em. I catch 'em and love 'em all the time."

Mama Girl was very serious when she said, "She used to *hop* around like a frog, too, though. On purpose, I mean."

The door buzzed and Miss Cranshaw said, "That'll be Mike. I asked him to come by as soon as he could."

She opened the door and Mike McClatchey came in.

"Kate," he said, "I don't think anything has made me as happy as your conviction that the play will fail."

Then he said hello to Mama Girl and me. He received a cup of tea from Miss Cranshaw, and he said, "That means only one thing to *me*—that you really like the play. And if you like it, I want to produce it—with your help."

"Well," Miss Cranshaw said, "we've been talking about it."

"Is Twink the one to do the little girl?" Mike said.

"Oh, I suppose there are any number of little girls who have had a lot of experience," Miss Cranshaw said, "and might be easier to work with."

"Will you work with *her?*" Mike said.

"I *have* been working with her."

"What do you think?"

"She's the girl."

Mike McClatchey looked at Mama Girl and said, "Well, what are we waiting for? Let's get happy, shall we?"

"She hasn't said she *wants* to be the little girl," Mama Girl said.

Mike McClatchey looked at me and said, "But you *do*, don't you?"

"Yes, I do," I said, "but I can't. I don't know how."

"Miss Cranshaw will teach you how."

Mama Girl said to me, "Well, how about it, Frog? It's up to you."

"I could *try*, but my father would have to say I could first."

"All right," Mike McClatchey said. "Here's the phone. Call him."

Mama Girl took the phone and gave the hotel operator the number in Paris. We all waited for the operator to call back, and then she did, and Mama Girl handed me the phone and said, "All right, Frog. Talk to your father."

"Can I talk to my brother, too?"

"Yes, of course," Miss Cranshaw said, so I talked to my father, and then to my brother, and then to my father again, and I was about to say good-by when Mama Girl said, "Let me speak to them, too, will you, Frog?"

Mama Girl spoke to them, and then she said to my father, "She was supposed to ask your permission to appear in a play, but she forgot to."

Then Mama Girl answered a lot of questions about the play, and then she handed me the phone again and she said, "You ask him, Frog."

I said, "Can I?"

My father said "Do you *want* to?"

"Yes."

"Really?"

"Yes."

"All right, then," my father said. "Ask your mother to please send a copy of the play to me by airmail. I'll read it and wire her. In the meantime, you can go along as if I had said O.K., but I *do* have to read it first, Twink."

"All right, Papa," I said. "When are you coming home?"

"Well, I feel at home right *here,*" my father said, "but of course I miss you very much." And then in a soft voice he said, "I miss your mother, too, but please don't tell her, will you?"

"All right, Papa."

"Pete wants to talk to you again."

My brother Peter Bolivia Agriculture came on the line again and he said something in French. Then he said, "That means why don't you and Mama come to Paris?"

I said, "I can't. What you doing, Pete?"

"Oh, studying most of the time, but having a lot of fun, too. Of course I practice the piano every day. I've composed a few little pieces. I'll play them for you some day. Did you know Pop composed a whole piano concerto when he was my age? I'm going to do one, too, before my next birthday. Good-by, Twink. If you get a chance, catch one of the games in the American League. They're having a great race."

"All right, Peter," I said. "I will. Good-by."

I hung up and told everybody what my father had said, and I told Mama Girl to please send him a copy of the play by airmail, so Mike McClatchey brought a copy of the play out of his brief case, and a big brown envelope. Mama Girl wrote my father's address on the envelope, Mike put the play inside and sealed it. He said the play would be on its way within an hour, and with luck it would be in Paris tomorrow.

"In the meantime, what do you think?" he said. "Do you think your father will say O.K.?"

"Yes," I said.

Mike smiled and said, "Do you know, Kate, I honestly believe this play is going to be a hit?" Everybody laughed, and then he said, "I've got to run."

"So do we," Mama Girl said.

"Where to?"

"A long walk," Mama Girl said. "In the streets this time."

We said good-by and thanks very much to Miss Cranshaw, and we went to the elevator with Mike McClatchey.

"I'm absolutely delighted," Mike said. "And please don't be worried—about *anything.* I'm having supper with Emerson tonight. I'm going to say there's a good chance we've found the girl. And then I'm going to wait for him to take it from there. I know he'll want to meet her—and of course her mother. Keep breakfast open tomorrow, will you?"

"Breakfast is *always* open tomorrow," Mama Girl said.

Mike jumped into a taxi on Fifth Avenue and Mama Girl and I began to walk—in the streets this time.

Chapter 17

In This Corner
Gladys Dubarry

*B*efore I knew it a whole week went by. I don't think I'll *ever* remember all of the things that happened. My father received the play and read it, but instead of sending a telegram he telephoned. He and Mama Girl had a long talk, and then he said to me, "If you really want to do it, Twink, go ahead, because it *is* a beautiful play, and some day I'll make an opera out of it."

Mama Girl told Mike McClatchey O.K., and then one day my father talked to Mike about the play, and my father agreed to compose music for it.

Mike asked him to come to New York, but my father didn't want to do that.

Other things happened, too.

The morning after the Big Tea at Miss Cranshaw's Mike McClatchey and the man who wrote the play, Emerson Tully, had breakfast at the Pierre with Mama Girl and me, and that afternoon Mike telephoned Mama Girl and told her that Emerson liked us both very much, and that he was going to write the whole play over again, because he wanted Mama Girl to play the little girl's mother.

So then Mama Girl was very happy, and she said, "Now, Frog, we've both got to be professionals, we've got to work and work and work, and I know we're going to have more fun than ever before."

That evening we took a taxi to Mike's offices on Fifth Avenue and some of Mike's staff were there, and his lawyer. Mike and Mama Girl went over the contracts, which we would sign as soon as we got word from my father. I never saw my mother so excited and happy, or so surprised. Afterwards she said, "Why, Frog, they're treating you like a star, that's what they're doing."

"*You're* the star," I said. "You're the real star."

"You'll be rich," Mama Girl said, "and it won't be so bad for me, either. Of course I'll be spending a lot of money, but almost all of yours will go into a trust. I certainly am glad we're friends."

"Friends?" I said. "You're a lot more than a friend to me, Mama Girl. If it hadn't been for you, I wouldn't even have been born."

"Your father had something to do with it."

"If you hadn't met him and married him, where would I be right now?"

"Well, it's too late to get yourself unborn," Mama Girl said. "Your father's your father, your mother's your mother, and you're you—nothing can *ever* change that. But you're going to be a star, too—all on account of Mother Viola."

"What's she got to do with it?"

"Everything. If she'd come to Macaroni Lane on time, I would have gone to Clara Coolbaw's dinner party, and we wouldn't have come to New York."

"Oh, yes. I forgot. We've got to write to Mother Viola and thank her."

"I'll *thank* her!" Mama Girl said. "She had her nerve not coming!"

"Aren't you glad she didn't?"

"Of course, but I don't like help you can't depend on."

"Maybe she got sick, or her children, or grandchildren."

"She should have phoned. I'm very angry at her."

Every day things were lively and exciting, and every night Mama Girl and I talked and remembered, but I'll never be able to remember *everything* because so many things happened so quickly after my father said I could go on the stage.

First, I began to work very hard with Miss Cranshaw. Mama Girl and I went to her apartment at eight every morning, and we worked until ten. Miss Cranshaw taught us how to stand, how to walk, how to dance, how to pick up things, how to look at them, how to speak, only there are *thousands* of ways to speak.

Miss Cranshaw gave us our schedule. We got up at six every morning. We walked in the Park half an hour, then we had breakfast at the Pierre—a big one for me, and a little one for Mama Girl, because Miss Cranshaw wanted her to take off a few pounds.

"I don't want you to become a bag of bones," she said, "but I *do* want you to be as swift as Frog, because that is absolutely necessary in the play. You and Frog must become almost the same person—more than you already are, and of course in terms that an audience can understand. And you can't do that if you're all round and roly from eating, and frustration, and anxiety. You haven't got anything to be anxious about anymore, except the one thing I want you *always* to be anxious about—your part in the play."

After breakfast every morning in the Coffee Shop at the Pierre we went up to 2109, and Mama Girl read a little of the play, over and over, and I listened. Miss Cranshaw didn't want me to begin practicing my lines until I had heard my mother read them many times—until I almost knew them by heart.

At half past seven we rested, but of course I couldn't. Sometimes Mama Girl took a nap, but I just stretched out and remembered things. Sometimes a little before eight Miss Cranshaw visited 2109.

The day Mama Girl signed all the papers at Mike McClatchey's office she said, "Well, Frog, we're in the money now."

When we got to the Pierre she spoke to the manager about an apartment. An hour later we moved in, and it was beautiful—on the thirty-third floor.

But, oh, what a mistake *that* was!

Miss Cranshaw went to 2109 the next morning, but of course we weren't there. She called the manager, and he told her we were in 3336 now, so Miss Cranshaw came up and paid us a visit. I thought she would be very happy about our new home, but she wasn't at all. She was angry, but she tried not to let Mama Girl know. She's a pro so, of course, she knows how to hide anger.

"This is one of the most beautiful apartments in the hotel," she said. "It used to be Mrs. Keegan's, but, do you know, it isn't *right* for you two at all. Oh, I know you can afford it now, but this just isn't a place to work, and of course when anybody is in a play, it is necessary to work all the time, night and day."

"But 2109 hasn't even got two *beds*," Mama Girl said.

"Of course," Miss Cranshaw said.

"I can't have friends to visit me there."

"Of course not."

"I feel happier here."

"I must speak plainly now," Miss Cranshaw said. "I don't think it's in order at the present time for you to be *that* happy. It's like trying to enjoy the rewards of an achievement before the achievement has been made. Plenty of time to enjoy fame and fortune. Now is the time to work, to be a little uncomfortable, to be a little anxious, all the time."

Mama Girl picked up the receiver and spoke to the manager, and an hour later we were back in 2109. I don't know why, but I was glad we were.

Gladys Dubarry came by with her personal doctor, and she began to make an awful fuss because we were still in such a small room.

"Why, the papers are full of reports of your wonderful luck," she said. "How can you possibly permit yourself to stay in a place like this?"

"You just listen to me a minute, please," Mama Girl said. "I've known you since we were both little girls. You've had a fortune all your life. You don't have to do anything but spend your money. You don't have to get married and try to make a life for yourself, so you *haven't* gotten married. You don't have to get divorced because your marriage hasn't worked out, because you haven't *been* married. You don't have to try to be a good mother to your son and your daughter after your family has broken up, because you haven't *got* a son and a daughter. You don't have to do anything but buy expensive clothes for yourself, expensive houses and apartments full of expensive things, and be thrilled to death all the time, because all *you've* got is your money and yourself, and as far as I'm concerned—if you're going to nag at *me*—you're *welcome* to them, but I'm going to live anywhere I please, any way I please, and this is where I want to live right now, and the way I want to live."

Gladys Dubarry said, "I'll never speak to you again as long as I live."

She turned to her personal doctor and began to cry.

Then she shouted at him, "Well, what the hell are *you* standing there for with your mouth open? If you're a doctor, take her temperature. You can see the poor girl's deathly sick, can't you? Sick—sick—sick! I've never seen her so sick."

He put his arms around Gladys Dubarry, and he said, "All right, now. All right, now, Dumpling."

Gladys Dubarry jumped out of his arms and screamed at him, "Don't you dare Dumpling me, you chiropractor, you fortune-hunter, you phony! Oh, I know you, Mr. Tall, Dark, Handsome, Sneaky, and Boring—I know you good! Don't you *ever* dare Dumpling me again."

Gladys Dubarry looked around at everybody, and then she began to stamp her feet and tear her handbag and scream. Her personal doctor brought a little box of pills out of his pocket and he said, "Miss Dubarry, please take two of these pills."

Gladys Dubarry knocked the little box of pills out of his hands. The box hit the ceiling and all of the little pills fell out. The doctor began to pick them up. The telephone rang and Mama Girl answered it.

"No," she said. "Nothing's the matter here at all. You can tell my neighbors I'm rehearsing, and I'm sorry if I've disturbed them. It won't happen again."

She hung up and looked straight at her old friend, and then she said, "You've got your nerve coming in here and screaming like a fishwife. You've scared the life out of my daughter."

"I'm not scared," I said.

"You see?" Gladys Dubarry said. "She's not scared at all. She knows perfectly well I've been terribly hurt—by my best friend. Well, if you're not my friend anymore, *she* is—aren't you, Frog?"

"I would rather you didn't ask her silly questions," Mama Girl said.

"I came to tell you both how happy I am for you," Gladys Dubarry said. "I came to be thrilled for you. I'm sorry if a little success has changed you so quickly from a sensitive friend into a brutal enemy."

The doctor stepped up to Gladys Dubarry and put out his hand with two little pills in it.

"What's that?" Gladys Dubarry said.

"Sedative," the doctor whispered.

Gladys Dubarry knocked the pills out of his hand. The two little pills hit the ceiling, and broke.

"*You* take them!" she said, but now she wasn't screaming any more. "I don't need any sedatives, you fortune-hunting phony. And they're not sedatives, anyhow. If they were I wouldn't be so excitable. I've taken six or seven a day for a whole year now. They're chalk—that's what they are. Just chalk. Well, I don't like *chalk!*"

The doctor bowed to Mama Girl, and then to me, and he turned to go.

"Where do you think *you're* going?" Gladys Dubarry said. The doctor stopped at the door. He turned, and then he just looked at her a long time. He didn't say anything. He opened the door and went out.

Gladys Dubarry looked at her handbag, all tattered and torn, but she didn't cry.

"Why don't you marry him?" Mama Girl said. She spoke very softly.

"Why should I?" Gladys Dubarry said. She spoke very softly, too.

"Well, for one thing, he loves you," Mama Girl said.

Gladys Dubarry didn't look at Mama Girl. She just kept straightening out her handbag.

"Do you really think so?" she said.

"Of course he does. I saw *that* the first time I saw him."

"I can't stand a man who lets himself be pushed around by a woman," Gladys said.

"His mother?" Mama Girl said.

"No," Gladys Dubarry said. "Not his mother. *Me.* His *mother* adores him. She despises me."

"Marry him."

"He's not a fortune-hunter at all. I just said that. I was angry. But he just doesn't know how to treat a girl like me."

"Teach him how."

"What do you think I've been trying to do for a whole year?"

"How do you *want* him to treat you?"

"I want him to treat me like a girl. I don't want him to listen to everything I say, and do everything I ask him to do. He's got to *make* me marry him."

"*You* make him make you marry him."

"How?"

"I don't know, but I'm sure *you* do."

"I'm afraid."

"Of what?"

"Of making a mistake."

"Sometimes it's a mistake *not* to make a mistake, you know."

"I'm afraid he'll poison me."

"What for?"

"My fortune."

"Oh, come off it, will you?" Mama Girl said. "You and your fortune. You're the poorest girl in New York."

"I really *am*, am I not?"

"Of course you are. Forget your fortune, and marry him."

"Are you sure he won't poison me?"

"Why should he?"

"If he treated me the way I treat him and we were married, I'd poison *him.*"

"Stop treating him that way."

"I can't. I *want* to, but I just can't."

"Maybe you'd better see a psychiatrist."

"Do you know a good one?"

"Of course not, but *he* does."

"I wouldn't want him to know about a thing like that. I'm afraid of having children, too."

"Oh, get out of here, will you, please?" Mama Girl said, but she didn't say it angry.

"I'll go," Gladys Dubarry said, "but just remember one thing—I'm not talking to you again as long as I live."

"O.K.," Mama Girl said.

Gladys Dubarry went to the door.

"From now on I'll *write* to you," she said, "and don't you dare ever speak to me again, either—just write if you really want to."

"O.K."

"Good-by, Frog," she said. "I love you, and I always will."

"I love you, too," I said.

"I know you do, Frog, and I know it isn't because you want me to remember you in my will, but I'm *going* to, just the same."

"Oh, get out of here," Mama Girl said.

"I'm glad you're famous now," Gladys Dubarry whispered, "but I'm awfully sorry it's gone to your head. I never believed you'd drop your best friend like a hot potato the minute you got famous."

"I'm *not* famous," Mama Girl said. "And sometimes you can be just about the biggest bore in the world."

"Perhaps there's a very good one in Vienna," Gladys Dubarry said. "I'll *send* for him."

"Sure, sure—big deal."

"I've got to have the *best*, don't I?"

"Go on downstairs and ask the desk to let you have the classified telephone directory," Mama Girl said. "Find the listing for psychiatrists. Find the one whose office is nearest your house. Phone him. Tell him your name's Gladys Smith, so you'll be able to tell him the truth about yourself. It's the only way you'll ever be able to pick yourself up out of a whole lifetime of delusions of grandeur."

"I haven't one single delusion of grandeur."

"Oh, no? Well, just try living without your fortune for a month. You'll find out what you've got and what you haven't got. Give yourself fifty dollars to live on in a little room somewhere until you find a job."

"I could take a room just like this one—right here at the Pierre," Gladys Dubarry said. "Will you speak to the manager and tell him you've got a friend who's very poor and *must* have a room like this one until she finds a job?"

"I will not."

"I'm not speaking to you again as long as I live," Gladys Dubarry said. "Fame will pass, but friendship *never* will. I know you'll be sorry and ashamed when you come to me for help, and instead of turning you away I'm going to help you. Good-by forever."

"Good-by forever," Mama Girl said.

Gladys Dubarry went out.

Mama Girl picked up the play and began to read again, as if nothing had happened. Her voice was better now than ever. I listened, but I couldn't help thinking about Gladys Dubarry. I wished she wouldn't be so unhappy. The door buzzed. Mama Girl opened it, and there was Gladys Dubarry again, holding out a roll of currency.

"I happened to find this money in my handbag," she said, "and I'd like Frog to have it to spend on herself for clothes and an automobile *before* I'm dead."

Mama Girl pushed her hand away, but she wasn't angry, and she said, "Oh, go away, will you?"

She shut the door, and went right on reading.

It was one thing after another all the time—people, talk, work, study, walk, eat, sleep, wake up. I can't ever hope to remember every little bit of it, but it was all fun, because Mama Girl was happy.

In spite of the hard work, she was happy. In spite of the friends she had, like Gladys Dubarry, who were always visiting her, or asking her to visit them, or telephoning and talking, she was happy—or maybe it was on *account* of them. I don't know.

All I know is that for the first time in a long time she was happy. Not just happy for a few minutes now and then, and then very unhappy, but happy all the time.

The way she woke up every morning was different now, even. She couldn't *wait* to get up, and that had never happened before, because she had always hated to get up, she had always hated to get her own cup of coffee. I had had to learn how to make coffee and take her a cup.

But now when the telephone rang at six in the morning, she knew what it was, a new day, a whole new day of fun, and she jumped out of bed, answered the phone, said thank you, jumped into a tub, called me, we bathed, and then we got dressed.

We went to the Park, and it was just wonderful, because everything she did she *wanted* to do, she couldn't wait to do. Everything was on purpose now, instead of *not* on purpose. Mama Girl knew what she was doing, and why. She had a purpose, and she *liked* the purpose. Of course she had to work hard, every day, almost every hour of every day, but she was excited about the work, and she loved it, and so it wasn't really work, it was fun.

Sometimes Miss Cranshaw would stop suddenly and smile and say to her, "Do you know, I almost believe the play *is* going to be a hit, and I think it's on account of your part, and the way you're going at it. I have an idea you are going to be O.K."

"But not nearly as good as Frog," Mamna Girl said.

"Well, let's not expect the *impossible*," Miss Cranshaw said, but of course we knew she was joking.

The only time I ever saw Miss Cranshaw angry at Mama Girl was when she explained to her that it was necessary for Mama Girl and me to live in 2109. But she was very nice about *that*, even. Mama Girl and I talked about it, and we know why Miss Cranshaw wanted us out of 3336 and back in 2109.

"It's better for the play, that's why," I said.

"Of course," Mama Girl said, "and to tell you the truth I prefer it, anyhow. And of course I save a lot of money, too."

Miss Cranshaw asked Mama Girl to spend as much time with me as possible, to go to as few places as possible without me. Mama Girl and I talked about that, too. The reason for that was the same reason, of course.

But Miss Cranshaw said that once a week, on Saturday night, Mama Girl must go to a party and have fun and talk a lot and stay up late, but only once a week.

She said that every Sunday I must go to the Park alone and stay there alone from noon until three o'clock—and I loved it. From the Park I could see the Pierre all the time, and I could guess where 2109 was. I knew Mama Girl was up there, still asleep because she had been to a Saturday-night party and hadn't gotten to bed until three in the morning, or four, or five. I made friends with boys and girls, and we played games. I had three dollars to spend any way I wanted to—with strict orders about lunch at one o'clock. I was to go to the cafeteria near the Zoo and order a cheese sandwich and a dish of strawberries or some other fruit, and then I was to have a pint of milk, and I was to take my time eating. I was not to have candy, but I could buy my friends candy and peanuts and popcorn until my money ran out, but it never did. I always took home at least a dollar, and sometimes two. Mama Girl kept it for me. She kept books, too. I mean, she did bookkeeping, to keep track of our money.

One evening Mama Girl and I were walking down Fifty-seventh Street to Fifth Avenue and I said, "What day is this?"

"Tuesday," Mama Girl said. "Why?"

"How long have we been in New York?"

"Well, we left California a week ago yesterday."

"Did the man take the money, or try for more?"

"The man who knows about opera?"

"Yes."

We came to the store with the television in the window. A little crowd of people was in the street watching again. We stopped to watch, too. After a while the man came there and he said he had spoken to his daddy in Italy. He had always minded his daddy, and his daddy had asked him to keep what he had, and not try for any more, and so he did.

We both wanted to know what the $64,000 question would have been, and if he would have been able to answer it, but of course we'll *never* know now.

One night Mike McClatchey telephoned and woke us up. Mama Girl talked on the phone a long time. When she stopped we were both wide-awake, because I can't sleep when somebody in the same room is talking.

"What's the matter?" I said.

"It's very important," Mama Girl said. "At noon tomorrow you and I are going to meet some people at Mike's office."

"What people?"

"Newspaper writers, magazine writers, and photographers. They're going to talk to us, and take pictures. Mike's going to try to have Miss Cranshaw there later on, and he would like her to invite a few special ones to visit her apartment, for tea."

"What for?"

"Publicity. It's one of the most important things in the theater. In the whole world. Even kings and queens hire people to get them publicity."

"Why?"

"Everybody wants people to know *good* things about them."

"Are the things true?"

"Well, not always, or not *absolutely* true, but a good publicity man can make almost anybody seem to be a nice person. He could make a bank robber seem nice if he wanted to."

"How?"

"Well, he would talk to the bank robber, and he would find something in the bank robber's life that was nice. He would build it up, and send it to the newspapers. They would print the story, and it would tell all about the bank robber when he was a small boy in Missouri and went to Sunday school and was kind to his mother and things like that."

"Would everybody forget that he robbed the bank?"

"Well, they might not forget it, but they wouldn't feel so badly about it, either. And then somebody in Hollywood would phone him, and make an appointment to talk to him about making a movie out of the story of his life."

"What are they going to write about *us?*"

"Well, of course with us it's different. It's not the way it is with a bank robber at all."

"What way *is* it?"

"Oh, it'll be a lot of fun. They're all nice men and women. They want to meet us and take pictures, first at Mike's office, then here at 2109, then at Miss Cranshaw's, then in the Park, and so on."

"*Why,* though?"

"Because right now you and I, Frog, we're news. We're *big* news in the world of the theater."

"Since when?"

"Since Mike McClatchey went to work, and you and I went to work, and Miss Cranshaw went to work."

"Weren't we *always* news?"

"Of course we were, but not the way we are now. We're in a Mike McClatchey play. It's going to be one of the most important plays of the new season. We're news because we're not famous yet, and may be famous after the play opens."

"Will we *know* if we are?"

"I'll say we will! *We'll* know, and everybody else will, too."

"Will we be different?"

"Of course we will. When you do a good job, and everybody likes it, and you earn money, then you *are* different, you're not the same at all."

"Let's go to sleep," I said.

"Yes," Mama Girl said.

Chapter 18

Ladies and Gentlemen of the Press

*M*ike McClatchey's office is in a big building on Fifth Avenue between Forty-ninth and Fiftieth, and it's on the fiftieth floor. You can see the East River from up there, and the boats, and the bridges. You can see a lot of New York, too. I've been there in the morning, and I've been there at night, after dark, when all the lights of the city go on. Everything is good to see from up there, night or day. There are five rooms, and one of them is very big, Mike's. The others are for his secretaries and other workers.

When Mama Girl and I opened the door of the first office, Helen Gomez, who is Mike's private secretary, was waiting for us.

"Everybody's in Mr. McClatchey's office," she said.

"I'm scared," Mama Girl said.

"Don't be," Helen Gomez said. "You both look wonderful. The whole town's buzzing about you two and the play. I've read it ten times, I guess, but I can't wait to see the new version. Have you seen it?"

"Oh, no," Mama Girl said, "but I'm dying to."

"I understand it's finished, but he wants to work on it some more. He feels it's a much better play now."

"It's wonderful just the way it is."

"Yes, but just think how much more wonderful it's *going* to be. You'd better go in."

"I don't know what to say," Mama Girl said.

Helen Gomez laughed. "Don't give it a thought. You'll do all right, don't worry about *that.* This whole office has come to life since you two came to town."

"You're very sweet, Helen."

"I'm not being sweet. I'm telling you the truth. Mr. McClatchey and Emerson Tully sat and talked about the play for weeks before you arrived. They just couldn't decide how to do it, and half the time Mike—Mr. McClatchey—wasn't sure he *would* do it. This place is no fun at all if Mr. McClatchey isn't producing. He's a natural-born producer. He's got to be producing to be happy. I've been with him ten years and I've never seen him so happy."

Helen Gomez smiled at me and she said, "I happen to know it's on account of you, young lady, and your beautiful mother. I *hear* things, you know."

"Helen," Mama Girl said, "I don't want to keep them waiting, but please help me. You've had a lot of experience. Nothing like this has ever happened to me before. Now, really, what do I do?"

"You want *me* to tell *you* what to do?" Helen Gomez laughed. "I came from Arizona fifteen years ago to be a great actress. Well, here I am, and *glad* to be here, too. I'd go home in two minutes if I didn't work for Mike—Mr. McClatchey. Believe me, you don't have a thing to worry about."

"Helen, you're the sweetest girl in the whole world,"

Mama Girl said. "I know you've put in a good word for us
with Mike—Mr. McClatchey."

"You bet your sweet life I have," Helen said, "because I
don't want to be out of a job I've had so long. And unless
Mr. McClatchey has a hit in this play, somebody just *has*
to go. Well, I've read every manuscript that's come into
this office, and this one's a beaut—but it needed something. It needed you. Both of you. Now go on in there
and just let them look at you."

"Shall I be serious?" Mama Girl said.

"Be any way you like. It's all right. Hurry now. Mr.
McClatchey would be awfully annoyed with me if he knew
I had kept you here even an instant, and I don't like Mr.
McClatchey to be annoyed with me."

So Mama Girl and I smiled at Helen Gomez, and Mama
Girl squeezed her hand, and we went in.

There were a lot of men there, and three or four
women. Mike McClatchey jumped up from behind his
desk when he saw us and he hurried to Mama Girl and put
his arm around her, and his other arm around me, and we
all smiled, and a man with a camera said, "Could you hold
that, Mike?" So we didn't move, and the man pressed
something on his camera. There was a flash. He removed
the bulb quickly, and then two other men and a woman
with a camera flashed their cameras, too. And then Mike
said, "Plenty of time, ladies and gentlemen. Allow me to
introduce the star of my next play. I say the star, because
both of them *are* the star."

Mike introduced us to everybody one by one, and then
he invited everybody to help himself to food and drink
from the big table along the wall that was loaded with
bottles and glasses and a roasted turkey with a lot of it
carefully sliced, and a ham, and a big glass bowl full of
salad, and another full of fresh fruit, peeled and cut up,

and mixed together, and all kinds of other good things to eat.

"I think you two might as well know," an old man with a big smile said, "that as starved as we are—being newspapermen and women—we didn't touch anything because we wanted to eat and drink with you."

Everybody laughed and got a plate, and the old man said to Mama Girl, "Now, don't you worry about a thing. We like you."

He put his arms around us the way Mike McClatchey had done, and he squeezed, and then he said, "Mike has been trying to tell us about you, but of course we've had to wait— to *see* you, and make up our own minds. This isn't going to be hard work for you. It's going to be food and drink with friends. You know, newspapers and magazines *need* people like you. When the time comes to answer questions, just one word from an old-timer who's interviewed them all. Don't *try.* Because you don't *have* to. All right?"

"All right," Mama Girl said.

"All right?" the old man said to me.

"All right," I said.

He stopped squeezing, and went to where the bottles were, and quickly poured something out of a bottle into a glass, without ice. He looked for us, found us, and then he lifted the glass, smiled, and drank it all down. Then his old face became very serious, almost sad, and he put ice in the glass and poured again.

"I love him," Mama Girl whispered. "Whoever he is, I just love him, Frog, don't you?"

"He's Archie Palmer of the United Press."

"Frog," Mama Girl said, "you didn't remember the name of *everybody* Mike introduced us to, did you?"

"Oh, no," I said. "Just him, and Elizabeth Corbett of *Vogue.*"

"What made you remember *their* names?"

"They did. I like them. I like everybody, but them especially."

"Which one is Elizabeth Corbett?"

"Over there," I said, so Mama Girl and I went to her, and she saw us coming and waited for us.

"Well, now," she said, "how nice of you to come to speak to me."

"How nice of you to be here," Mama Girl said.

Miss Corbett handed each of us a plate, and Mama Girl and I put food on our plates, and Miss Corbett put food on hers, and we talked and laughed as we moved along the table.

I just couldn't understand it, it was so nice. It was so high up, up there, and everybody was so nice, I just didn't know why, but I was glad just the same. I was glad my father in Paris had said I could go on the stage, because if he hadn't I wouldn't have been up there. I was glad Mother Viola hadn't come to our house on Macaroni Lane in Pacific Palisades when she was supposed to, either, because if she had I would have been there still.

The only thing I wasn't glad about was that my friend Deb wasn't with me, because Deborah Schlomb is my best friend, and if anything good happens to me, I want it to happen to her, too.

Chapter 19

The New Play

*T*he eating, drinking, and talking kept up for a long time, and then all of a sudden everything quieted down.

Mike McClatchey said, "Ladies and gentlemen, you may now fire away."

One by one the ladies and gentlemen asked questions. They asked Mike, they asked Mama Girl, and they asked me. One or two of them wrote things down in notebooks, but most of them didn't. After about an hour some of the men and women thanked Mike and said good-by to Mama Girl and me, and went away.

Archie Palmer said, "You're in. If Mike *really* has a good play, as he *says* he has, if you can be as impressive in the play as you are anyhow, all is well."

Elizabeth Corbett said, "No matter what happens—and you know *anything* can happen in the theater—you're ahead of the game. If the play fails, if your performances are bad, if you just can't act, if the play doesn't even get to Broadway, if it closes out of town, just remember you're ahead of the game. Good-by."

"Oh, please," Mama Girl said. "Don't go. You've scared the life out of me. The play has got to be a hit. We've *got* to be great. *Everything* has got to be great. It's just got to, that's all."

Elizabeth Corbett smiled and patted Mama Girl's hand, and then she put my hand on Mama Girl's and patted them both.

"Of course, of course," she said, "but you'll be much more apt to *be* great in the play if you know it *can* be a flop, if you know you *can* fail to play your parts as they ought to be played. And you mustn't ever be unprepared for failure. It happens more often than success, but we all manage to move along just the same. You're awfully successful just as you are. Work very hard, but don't care too much. I know you understand what I'm saying, and why I've had to say it, even at a time like this, so full of confidence and expectation. Call me anytime."

She kissed us on the cheek and went quickly, and Mama Girl looked at me, and I knew she was awfully worried.

"Oh, Frog," she said, "what are we going to do? We just mustn't fail."

"Maybe we won't."

"What good is maybe?"

"Better than nothing."

"Oh, I'm worried," Mama Girl said.

Emerson Tully came in, and Mike introduced him to the people who were still there. Some more pictures were taken, and a little later Miss Cranshaw came in, and some more pictures were taken with her, too.

But Mama Girl was upset, and it made me nervous.

"You stop being upset," I whispered.

"I can't," Mama Girl whispered.

"You've got to. It makes you look bad."

"What shall I do?"

"Forget about failing."

"Yes, I *must* believe everything is going to be great, and I *will*."

She began to be happy and confident again, but every once in a while when I looked at her I saw that she was still worried. It almost made me angry at Elizabeth Corbett, only I knew she was right.

The whole day was spent with the writers and photographers—first at Mike's office, and then at 2109, then at Miss Cranshaw's, and then in the Park.

When it was all over, Mike McClatchey took us to dinner at "21," upstairs in a private room. We had steaks and salads. After dinner Mike said, "This is a very important day. First, because we've met the press and they like us. Second, because Emerson has just finished the new version of the play."

Emerson Tully smiled and Miss Cranshaw said, "Good for you, boy. And do you *like* it?"

"Well," Emerson said, "of course not—nothing a man ever writes is good enough, but I think it is now a much better play than it was."

"Well, when do we get to read it?" Miss Cranshaw said.

"It'll take a few days to have it typed," Emerson said.

"In the meantime," Mike said, "suppose Emerson reads it to us?"

"Oh," Mama Girl said. "Do you mean you've got the manuscript *with* you?"

"Oh, yes," Emerson said.

Emerson Tully didn't carry a briefcase, the way Mike did. He didn't look or act like a playwright, either. If you saw him in the street, you'd never guess he was a man who could sit down and write a play. He was very young, and he looked like a football player. He had very broad shoulders, and very big hands. His feet were very big, too. His voice was strong, and sometimes loud, too—but not on purpose.

Emerson Tully reached into the back pocket of his trousers and brought out a manuscript folded in half. He spread it out in front of him on the table.

"I'm not a good reader," he said. "Mike, don't you think *you'd* better read it?"

"No," Mike said. "I want you to read it. I'll be busy *thinking,* as you read. Is everybody comfortable?"

Everybody was, of course, and excited, too.

"It'll take about two hours," Emerson said.

"Let's all just listen very carefully," Miss Cranshaw said, "and not discuss it until after it has been read."

"O.K.," Emerson said, "but before I begin I want Twink to know why I wrote this play." He looked at me and smiled, and then he became very serious, and he said, "I wrote it for you."

He had a goblet with brandy at the bottom of it. He took a sip, and smiled, and then he said, "Here goes, then."

He read the whole play from beginning to end, speaking in a clear voice. When he was finished nobody said a word, but Mama Girl blew her nose, and then she handed me the handkerchief and I blew my nose, too.

Mike McClatchey cleared his throat and rubbed his eyes, because he didn't want us to think he had tears in them, but he did.

Only Miss Cranshaw didn't have tears in her eyes. She said, "Young man, you have broken my heart. Mike, I think Mr. Tully may as well know I believed the first version would fail."

"Yes, that's true," Mike said to Emerson. "What do you think *now?*"

"I'm stumped," Miss Cranshaw said. "I can't even *guess.*

I'm afraid to. I know the play *should* be an event in the American theater. I even believe it should be a *hit*. But I'm just stumped. I don't know, that's all. And that means we've got to work very hard—harder than ever now."

Miss Cranshaw smiled at Mama Girl and said, "You especially, my dear, because now your part is just as important as Frog's, and how you do yours will determine how she will do hers. I'm still stunned, young man. Mike, is there anything more we ought to discuss?"

"There is, of course," Mike said, "but not tonight. If you'll let me have the manuscript, Emerson, I'll get it to Helen Gomez. She'll get it to somebody who'll mimeograph it—*tonight*. I'll have three copies at the Pierre tomorrow morning."

"Are you sure?" Miss Cranshaw said.

"Helen Gomez will take care of it, I know," Mike said. "Let's all read the play as soon as possible tomorrow morning, and then let's all get to work."

"Emerson," Mama Girl said, "thank you very much."

"Let me thank *you*," Emerson said.

"We'll study through August," Mike McClatchey said, "and then we'll cast the rest of the parts. We'll start rehearsals as soon as possible in September. We'll try out for two weeks in Philadelphia late in September, and from there we'll go to Boston for two more weeks. We'll open in New York early in November, at the Belasco, most likely."

"Then, my work is finished, is that right?" Emerson said.

"It's just beginning," Mike said. "I want you to direct the play."

"I don't know how to direct," Emerson said.

"I don't think anybody else in the whole world can bring this play in," Mike said.

"Mike," Emerson said, "I tell you I just don't know how to direct a play."

"I want you to *learn* while you're directing this one," Mike said.

"Miss Cranshaw," Emerson said, "believe me, I think Mike is making a mistake."

"I'm sure he *isn't*," Miss Cranshaw said. "Now, just don't worry about anything."

"Besides," Mike said, "don't forget you've got Kate Cranshaw to help you. Hasn't he, Kate?"

"I'll stay with the play all the way," Miss Cranshaw said.

We got up then. I was kind of excited and sleepy at the same time. Miss Cranshaw said she wanted to walk home, so Mike McClatchey put Mama Girl and me into a taxi, and he said, "Now go straight to bed, and be very happy, and be sure you don't worry about anything. I've noticed a little anxiety in your eyes all afternoon. Why?"

"Oh, Mike," Mama Girl said, "I'm thrilled to death, but it *is* an awful responsibility."

"I'm glad you think so," Mike said. "You're going to be great. Good night, now."

So we went home to 2109, and Mama Girl got me to bed, and then she sat on the bed and began to sing softly. Just hearing her sing made me sing, too, and then I fell asleep.

Chapter 20

Stage Fright

I was wide-awake before the telephone rang at six in the morning. Mama Girl answered it and then got back under the covers. I waited for her to say something and get up, but then I saw that she had gone back to sleep. I woke her up, and she said, "What is it, Frog?"

"We've got to get up."

"Why?" she said. It didn't seem possible, but she had forgotten *everything*. It seemed as if she didn't even know we were in New York.

I woke her up again.

"Mama Girl, don't you remember?"

"Remember what?"

"Emerson Tully—"

"Who's he?"

"The man who wrote the play."

"What play?"

"Oh, Mama Girl, wake up, will you?"

Mama Girl sat up.

"What's the matter, Frog?" she said. "I know something's the matter. What is it?"

"You won't wake up," I said.

She looked around at the walls of 2109, and I saw that now at last she *did* remember. I expected her to jump up and start a new day, but instead she just looked at me and groaned.

"Oh, Frog," she said. "What am I going to do?"

"Get up," I said.

"I'm scared."

"Mama Girl," I said, "you get up this minute, and stop being silly."

"I'm *not* being silly. I want to go home."

"You *can't* go home. We're in a play. Emerson Tully wrote the whole play over again. He did all that work for us—for *you.*"

"I want to go home and forget all about it."

"You get up!" I shouted. I *really* shouted, and Mama Girl jumped out of bed. It almost scared me.

"I'm up," she said. "I'm up, Frog. I'm sorry. I didn't sleep a wink all night. Everything went wrong. I couldn't act. I couldn't do my part at all. I spoiled the whole play. It was an awful flop, and the critics said it was all my fault. I was disgraced forever. I'm up, Frog, but I'm scared to death."

"It was just a bad dream," I said. "You'll feel much better after you have a bath, after we walk in the Park. We've got to read the play."

"Yes, I know."

"Well, aren't you going to draw a bath?"

"Yes, Frog, and thank you very much for being my pal."

She went to the bathroom, and then I heard the water pouring out of the tap into the tub. She came back to put out our clothes for the day.

"Are you still scared?"

"That's the trouble," she said. "I'm wide-awake now. I

know I'm not dreaming anymore. I know it's not a bad dream anymore but I'm *still* scared, only more than ever."

"Why, Mama Girl? It's what you've always wanted to do, isn't it?"

"Oh, yes, Frog. It's *more* than what I've always wanted. It's the biggest chance of my life. I'll never get another chance like this. And it's all on account of you, too. Only I can't stop being scared. After all, I haven't got any real experience, and it *is* a very big part, in a very special play. Mike could get the most famous actress in America to play the part. I just don't think I'm ready for a big part like that."

"You've *got* to be ready."

"Of course I've got to be ready, but I'm not, that's all. I'm just not."

"You cut that out," I said.

"You *will* help me, won't you, Frog? You won't let me be discouraged, will you?"

We got in the tub together, and then we got dressed, and went downstairs. At the desk Mama Girl asked if there was a package for us, but there wasn't.

We walked in the Park, very fast because Mama Girl was excited. Most of the time when she's excited she talks, but this time she didn't say one word until we got back to the Pierre.

"I'm all right now," she said. "I'm still scared, but I just don't care about that. I'm going to work very hard. I'm going to do the best I can. If Emerson Tully thinks I can do the part, if Mike McClatchey thinks I can, if Kate Cranshaw thinks I can, then it doesn't matter if I think I *can't*—I've *got* to, and I'm *going* to, that's all."

I was glad, but I was just as scared as she was, only I couldn't let her know. We went to the hotel desk again. The man there didn't even wait for us to ask if a package

had come, he just held it out to Mama Girl. We took it to
the Coffee Shop, we sat down at a table, and Mama Girl
brought two brand-new copies of the play out of the
envelope. There was a typed note clipped to the blue
cover of each copy. They were from Helen Gomez.

Mama Girl read hers: "Oh, what a beautiful part, and
just right for you! Love! Helen."

I read mine: "Twink, aren't you glad your beautiful
Mama is going to have such a wonderful part in your play?
Love. Helen."

"My play?" I said.

"Yes," Mama Girl said. "Everybody thinks of it as your
play. After all, the little girl is the most important person
in the play."

This made me *very* scared, but I just couldn't let Mama
Girl know.

We sat at the breakfast table a long time, but it wasn't
because we were eating, it was because Mama Girl was
reading a page of the play, thinking about it, and asking
questions about it. Sometimes she would look worried,
and then sometimes she would look confident.

Rosie the waitress came over and said, "Now, look
here, you two, eat your breakfasts."

She laughed, because Mama Girl began to eat very
quickly.

"I was only kidding," Rosie said.

"You *think* you were," Mama Girl said.

"I did it for a laugh. Another thing I do is go up to
people who are thinking or dreaming and say 'Boo.' "

"Don't ever do it to *me*," Mama Girl said. "Things like
that scare me, and I'm no good for two or three days,
because I keep expecting it to happen again."

"Really?"

"Yes. I'm sensitive."

"How about you, Twink?"

"I am, too," I said. "If somebody whispers 'Boo' in my ear, I get very scared."

"I won't do it, then," Rosie said. "But I never saw two people sit at a table with food in front of them and let it get cold the way you've done. I'm going to bring everything again—*hot.*"

"No, Rosie," Mama Girl said. "This is fine."

We were eating away, but Rosie just didn't like the food being cold, and of course it was. Scrambled eggs and crisp bacon with home-fried potatoes for me, because I love 'em, but not for Mama Girl, because Miss Cranshaw wants her not to be roly. We were almost finished when Rosie just picked up our plates and took them away, so Mama Girl went back to work on the play. Before we knew it, Rosie was back with scrambled eggs and bacon all over again.

"My treat," Rosie said. "Now, just please eat this nice food while it's hot."

"All right, Rosie," Mama Girl said, "and thank you very much."

We ate the food while it was hot—two breakfasts instead of one, one cold and one hot, and then Mama Girl asked Rosie to just keep pouring hot black coffee into her cup, because she wanted to work—right there.

"Just let me know when it's five minutes to eight," she said.

While Mama Girl worked I watched and listened. I counted the cups, too. Six cups of black coffee, but it didn't make her nervous, it made her calm. She smoked one Parliament after another, too.

"I'm glad you're not scared anymore," I said.

"Oh, but I *am*, Frog—but I'm working and when I'm working I haven't got time to *remember* that I'm scared.

I've just got to know what I'm doing, and why, and then I've just got to do it *better* than the greatest actress in the world."

"You will, Mama Girl."

"I'll *try*. I'll try like the girl trying to swim the English Channel, like the one walking the tightwire in the circus, like the one who's just got married."

"Who?"

"The girl who's just got married."

"Does *she* have to try, too?"

"Harder than anybody," Mama Girl said. "Unless of course she happens to marry somebody who doesn't expect anything from her at all."

"Mama Girl, is it as hard as all that to be a woman?"

"Yes, it is, Frog. I ought to know. That's why I'm scared. I didn't do good as a wife at all. If the drama critics had been called upon to review my work, I'm afraid I would have got an awful panning—and I guess I would have deserved it, too."

"Why, Mama Girl? What did you do wrong?"

"Oh, the things I *did* I did right enough, I suppose. It's just that I didn't do very many things—except go dead, unless it was something for me—just *me!*"

"What about my father?"

"Oh, if the critics had been called upon to review his performance, he would have been panned, too, but that's none of my business. In a play or in anything else, everybody has got to play his own part. I played mine very badly, and it doesn't improve matters any that your father did, too."

"What did *he* do wrong?"

"Who knows? Just about everything, I guess, because a marriage *isn't* a three-act play."

"What is it?"

"It's a three-*million*-act play—the minute it begins, there just isn't any end, outside of death or divorce. I hate death, so I chose divorce."

"Did my father get mad when you did that?"

"He sure did. He went stark raving mad."

"Is he still mad?"

"Yes, he is—not the same way, maybe, but deeper."

"Are you mad?"

"Of course."

"At him?"

"Yes, Frog, at him, but mostly at myself."

"I don't understand marriage."

"Of course you don't."

"I don't think I understand *anything,* because you're my mother and my father's my father, and you love me and my father loves me, but you're mad at each other."

"It's not easy to understand, Frog. I don't understand it too well myself, but I know when I'm dying, and when I'm killing somebody else, too, and I don't like it, that's all."

"I guess you live and learn," I said, because Deb used to say that whenever we saw something strange in a movie, only Deb was making fun of what we saw. We were talking and working on the play when Rosie came and said, "That's it, girls—five minutes to eight."

We got up quickly, Mama Girl paid the check at the cashier's, and we went upstairs, and straight to Miss Cranshaw's.

Chapter 21

Gladys Dubarry, Girl Bride

*W*e had got on the airplane at the International Airport in Los Angeles at eleven o'clock at night on the first day of August.

On the last day of August Gladys Dubarry married her personal doctor. His name was Hobart Tuppence. She had gone to a psychiatrist whose office was next door to her house on East Seventy-seventh, and under the name of Gladys Smythe, instead of Smith, which she thought was just a little *too* plain, she had told him the story of her life—but instead of going to see him once a week, the way most people do, she had gone once a day, and sometimes twice. Gladys told Mama Girl all about it just before the marriage party, right after the ceremony.

"I just talked and talked," Gladys said. "That's how psychiatry works. You talk and talk, and little by little you decide who you want to be, and what you want to do. Well, I decided I wanted to be Gladys Dubarry, and to marry Ho. But of course I hadn't seen him since our fight in your apartment at the Pierre."

"My *room* at the Pierre," Mama Girl said.

"Yes," Gladys said. "So I said to Siggy—that's the psychiatrist—'please telephone Hobart Tuppence for me,' but he didn't. They never do, you know. They just listen. You're supposed to believe they're thinking about you, that they understand everything, but, believe me, they *don't*. I don't think they even *hear* what you say. They just give you an hour, and you are expected to pay them twenty-five dollars. But they don't do anything—at *all*. They're *there*, that's all, and you talk and talk, and decide for yourself. Well, I decided I wanted to be Ho's wife, so if Siggy wouldn't get him on the phone, I *would*. I dialed Ho's number, and of course he answered, because he doesn't have a secretary or a nurse. Don't you think he's the handsomest?"

"Yes, but what did you tell him?"

"Oh, you know," Gladys said. "After you've been analyzed you don't beat around the bush. I said O.K."

"What did *that* mean?"

"That meant O.K., I'd marry him."

"Had he ever asked *you* to marry him?"

"Well, not in so many *words*, because he hasn't been analyzed, but I've always known he *wanted* to—and I was right, because—well, we're married, aren't we?"

The party was at her home, which has five floors, and a penthouse. We were in the penthouse, because Gladys wanted to rest a minute before going down to the fifth floor to greet the most important people at the party. Hobart Tuppence was in the entrance hall on the ground floor, to greet *everybody*.

Mama Girl and I saw him there when we arrived.

"Up to the penthouse," he said, "She's alone there, waiting for you. You'll find the private elevator at the end of the hall on the left."

"I'm so happy for both of you," Mama Girl said, and she kissed Ho on the cheek.

"Well, I love her," he said, "but I'm afraid I don't know

what to do with her. She seems to get her way in everything, and for some reason I can't—"

"Little by little," Mama Girl said.

"Am I expected to use *force?*" Ho said quickly, because
some more people had just come in.

"Yes," Mama Girl said. "A *lot* of it—but little by little."

When Gladys was ready to join the party she stood at
the top of a curved marble staircase going down to the
fifth floor. She just stood there and waited. The whole big
room was full of people who were wearing fine clothes and
talking and eating and drinking. After a moment somebody looked up and saw her, and then *everybody* looked
up. Gladys began to move down the stairway very slowly
and carefully.

I began to follow her, when Mama Girl took my arm,
and drew me back.

"Oh, for God's sake," she said.

Six or seven photographers were taking pictures. One of
them had a great big moving-picture camera.

"Come on," Mama Girl said.

We went back into the penthouse, straight to the private
elevator, and got in.

"What's the matter?"

"We've got to get out of here."

"We can't," I said. "She'll be very upset."

"No," Mama Girl said. "She'll never know the difference."

Mama Girl pushed one of the buttons of the elevator,
the door slid shut, and then the elevator began to move
down, slowly. At each floor we heard a lot of noise. The
elevator stopped, the door slid open, and we got out.

The hall was jammed with people Mama Girl didn't
know, so she looked around for a back door, but there just
wasn't one. We decided to work our way through the
people to the street, but when we got to the stairway

going up to the second floor, the people carried us along with them, and up. There wasn't one person Mama Girl knew on the second floor. We tried to get out, but we got carried up to the third floor. There wasn't anybody we knew there, either. It was the same on the fourth floor. There must have been a hundred people on each floor, but on the fifth there must have been *two* hundred, and they were all admiring Gladys. She was talking at the top of her voice, and laughing, and flirting with every man there.

"We've *got* to get out of here," Mama Girl said. "It's the best party I've ever been at, but I only came because she said in her telegram that if I didn't, her marriage would fail and it would be my fault. I just didn't want to have *that* on my conscience. I only wanted her to know I was happy for her, but we've got to go now, we've got to get back to work."

There were a lot of people on the marble staircase going up to the penthouse, but we managed to get through them, and to the top. We were about to go into the penthouse and use the elevator again when Gladys saw us and waved.

"Oh, oh," I thought. "*Now*, we'll just *have* to stay."

Gladys stopped waving, though, and she began to flirt some more, so we went into the penthouse. We were on our way back to the private elevator when we saw somebody away over in the corner, standing at a little bar, drinking. It was Ho.

"What are *you* doing up *here?*" Mama Girl said.

"Drinking," Ho said. "I've taken all I can take for one day. Her friends didn't come to see *me*, I can tell you that. They thought I was the butler. They didn't come to see *her*, either. I don't know *why* they came. I don't know why I ever got into this, either. What kind of a woman is she, anyway?"

"Oh, now, look here," Mama Girl said. "Put that drink down and straighten yourself out. This party'll be over in a couple of hours, and you'll be alone with a very rare and lovely girl—*your* wife."

"What's this party *for?*"

"For fun," Mama Girl said. "Now, go on downstairs and *have* fun, the same as everybody else. They've all been married, so of course they're celebrating *their* marriage, and you should celebrate *yours.*"

"Why aren't *you* down there, then?" Ho said.

"I've been on every floor," Mama Girl said. "It's after five, and I have a rehearsal at half past. I'll be late as it is. I simply had to come by for an hour to wish you both well."

"My mother's down there on the ground floor, sur-rounded by strangers," Ho said. "She lost my father. I mean *here,* at the party, two minutes after they arrived. I don't know where *he* is. But I know where my wife is, and I know where I am—*nowhere,* that's where."

"Listen to me," Mama Girl said. "Now, please straighten yourself out and forget all about your mother. She's proba-bly having more fun than anybody else at the party. Forget your father, too. The place is loaded with beautiful girls and women. And I think you had better forget all about yourself, too. That's the only way to start a marriage. Just have fun—with strangers."

"I don't understand this kind of business," Ho said. "I'm thirty-seven years old. This is my first marriage. I've waited all this time because it takes a lot of time to *get* to be a doctor. And because marriage has always meant more to me than anything else in the world. Is *this* a marriage?"

"A marriage *party,*" Mama Girl said. "Believe me, this

is as good a way as any to launch a marriage, if you can afford it. You've got to stop being alone. That's the first thing. You'll have plenty of time to have her all to yourself soon enough. You'll be twosies before you know it. Now, I've got to go, but before I do, let me see you go downstairs to your wife."

"I'm lost down there."

"That's the proper place to get lost," Mama Girl said. "Not up here. You'll know how right I am tomorrow."

"I don't know how to be the husband of a crazy woman," Ho said. "*Is* she crazy?"

"Of course not," Mama Girl said. "She's just mixed up, and she's counting on you to straighten her out. You've been married—"

Ho looked at his wristwatch and said, "One hour and thirty-five minutes."

"Yes," Mama Girl said. "The sooner you start straightening her out the better."

"How do I do *that?*"

"Little by little," Mama Girl said, "beginning right now. Now, go downstairs to your wife and be her husband."

Ho put down his glass and made a face. Then he shook his head as if something was in it that he wanted to get out of there, and then he went to the door, opened it, and went out.

Mama Girl and I went to the elevator. When we got out on the ground floor, there weren't quite so many people there as before, and after a little while we got to the street. We walked to the corner and found a taxi there. We got in and went to the Pierre. From the lobby Mama Girl telephoned Miss Cranshaw to explain why we were a little late and then we went up. Mama Girl and Miss Cranshaw talked about the marriage party a few minutes, and then it was time to get to work.

Miss Cranshaw said, "We'll take it from the beginning of Act Two. The key is this—the mother says happy things but she isn't really happy. Vocal tone is what we are going to be concerned about now. Posture and movement and gesture will come later. All right, then, read."

"I think we know our lines," Mama Girl said.

"You do?" Miss Cranshaw said. "Good, and I may say that so far you are moving along much more effectively than any of us expected, or had a right to expect. I know you've lived every minute for the play. Well, that's the *only* way to live when you are *in* a play."

We worked for about an hour. The telephone rang, and it was Mike McClatchey. He wanted all of us to go to his office right away, so we did.

When Helen Gomez saw Mama Girl she winked and smiled, so we knew it was something special. When we went into Mike's office he was all smiles.

On his desk was a big stack of music, and I knew it was my father's, because one of the first things I ever saw was my father's music, just as he wrote it, and I know the way he writes notes and words.

"Well," Mike said, "the music came from Paris by airmail early this afternoon." He picked up the pile of manuscript. "Here it is. He's had the new version of the play only two weeks, and when I flew over and talked to him he said he was a slow worker, so naturally I didn't expect anything at all for another two or three weeks, or maybe even longer. When I saw all this music I was sure it couldn't be very good. I was terribly let down. I have always believed in the best, no matter how long it takes. That's why I've kept some of my plays out of town for three or four months. Now, I'm not the best pianist in the world, but I *can* read music, and play after a fashion, too. Well, I've played the whole thing straight through." Mr.

McClatchey smiled at me, and then he said, "Well, Twink, your father *has* written the music for the play. Kate, would you like to hear a little of it?"

"Don't ask silly questions," Miss Cranshaw said. "You know perfectly well the music has been on our minds from the beginning. I can't believe it's finished, but let's hear it."

"There's a lot of it," Mike said. "Certainly more than I bargained for. His letter says he wrote a great deal more than he knew we'd be able to use, but he thought he'd better, anyhow. We're going to have quite a job picking and choosing." Mike sat at the baby grand, and he said, "Page one. We might as well begin at the beginning."

Mike began to play the music my father had composed for the play. It was very quiet and thoughtful, and then it became so lively that I had to dance to it, as if it was my father at home playing a new piece, especially for me, when I was a little girl.

Miss Cranshaw walked around me as I danced, and Mike watched. Then he stopped playing, and went to Mama Girl.

"Well," he said, "how do you like it?"

"Very much," Mama Girl said.

Then Mike went to Miss Cranshaw.

"Kate?" he said.

"It's just right," Miss Cranshaw said, "but of course it makes new work for me. You saw Twink dancing, of course."

"Yes," Mike said.

"Well," Miss Cranshaw said, "that's going to be part of my work. I don't want to call in a choreographer unless I have to. The way she danced just now is the way I want her to dance in the play, but of course she doesn't know what she did, or how she did it. Do you, Twink?"

"No," I said. "But I've always danced to my father's music."

"I'll work something out," Miss Cranshaw said.

"I've sent for Oscar Bailey," Mike said. "I've asked him to play it straight through for us, so we can *really* hear it. I'm having him form a small band, to get the whole thing on tape, so we can listen to it, and decide what we are going to do with it, how much of it we're going to be able to use. Emerson's on his way, too. In the meantime, is anybody hungry? I'm starved."

He pressed a button and Helen Gomez came in and he said, "Helen, please have some food sent along, and of course the minute Oscar Bailey and Emerson get here, send them in."

Mike played the same music over again while we were waiting, and I danced again, and afterwards Miss Cranshaw said, "It's just as I thought. She dances a little differently each time, but I think it's all right. I think I'll want it to be that way at every performance."

Oscar Bailey was a very thin man. Everything about him was thin—his face, his neck, his arms, his fingers—but his eyes were very alive and almost a little mean—at least until you heard his voice, which was low and gentle. He turned the pages of my father's music, and then when Emerson Tully came in Oscar looked around and said, "If you're ready, I am."

"I've got some food coming," Mike said.

"Go right ahead while I'm playing," Oscar said. "I'll have some after I'm finished."

He sat down at the piano, and didn't do anything for a minute. And then he began to play, but he *really* played—much better than Mike, much better than my father, even. Miss Cranshaw kept watching me. I guess she was waiting for me to dance again, but I couldn't move. I just wanted to hear the music my father had written for the play. As Oscar Bailey played, everybody looked at one another and smiled and nodded, and when he was finished everybody applauded. He got up and didn't even smile.

"Wow," he said.

A few minutes later he said it again.

He was about an hour playing the music, but nobody moved the whole time. A few minutes after he was finished Helen Gomez pushed a table loaded with food into the office and Mike said, "What took you so long?"

"Do you think I'd interrupt *that* music?" Helen said.

"Did *you* hear it?" Mike said.

"I certainly did—over the interoffice," Helen said. "Well, here's food."

Helen took two or three little sandwiches, and began to eat them. The rest of us helped ourselves, as Mike McClatchey and Mama Girl and Oscar Bailey and Emerson Tully and Kate Cranshaw talked about the music my father had written.

I felt very proud, because he *is* my father, and he wrote the music.

Chapter 22

Memories of California, Fun at Coney Island

*T*he whole first month in New York was hot, but I didn't care, because I like it hot. I like it cold, too, but when it's hot I like it hot. I wear summer dresses then.

I like the snow, too, but in California we didn't see any. All we saw was sunshine, and a little rain once in a while.

Once there was a lot of rain, and I went to school in my raincoat with a summer dress underneath. The rain stopped at noon, though, and when I walked home with Deborah Schlomb the sidewalks were dry, and everything was the same as ever.

You don't get snow in California. You don't even get rain. All you get is California—day after day—and all I can say is I like it. It's fun. The smart-aleck blackbirds come down out of the trees onto the lawn and dig for things there, and when you go after them they don't fly away, they just *walk* away a little, and look at you. The mockingbirds stand in the eucalyptus trees and sing the songs of other birds. One mocker can go along for half an hour without singing two tunes twice. The little moles puff soft dirt up out of the ground, and if you're lucky you can see them when they stick their heads up, and then go back quickly. I never did see one of them all the way out. They don't like to be seen. The white butterflies spring up and down wherever things are growing, and they're growing everywhere, flowers, weeds, bushes, and trees. There are brown butterflies, too, and all kinds of moths, which are like butterflies but don't fly the same way, they go around as if they were lost and nervous in the daytime. There are lizards and bugs of all kinds, too. In the cool of the evening you'll see snails sticking out from their shells, with their feelers out. If you bend down and put your finger in front of one of them, just as soon as a feeler touches your finger, there he goes, the feelers go right back into his softness, and then all of the front and back slip under and inside the shell, and he stops moving. You can always see how far he has moved, because he leaves a thin line of his own self on the sidewalk. There are garden snakes, too, but the minute anybody sees one of *them,* you hear a lot of noise, because everybody is afraid of them. They go very fast when they hear a lot of noise, and you can look and never see them again.

Up the hill next to our house on Macaroni Lane were things to see all the time. It was twenty acres there of a private estate, with a big house for the owners, and a little one for the caretaker. They had six horses that they rode in a fenced-in place, or down the side of one hill into the valley, and up the side of the other. They had a flock of black-faced sheep, too, and there were always a few lambs going around with the sheep. You could hear them making the sound they make, like baa, or whatever it is. They had two collies, too, that used to come through the wire fence and visit the kids of Macaroni Lane. Even the horses used to come to the wire fence and stand there and watch the kids, and we used to watch them, too.

Another thing they had were six goats, which they kept chained where there was grass to eat. The goats used to stop eating to watch the kids, too.

There was a funny boy named Ned Gage who had a loud voice. One afternoon he saw the goats standing and looking at ten or eleven turkeys the people had bought for Thanksgiving. The goats just stood there and looked at the turkeys and listened to them talking and gobbling. Ned Gage stood at the end of Macaroni Lane and looked at the goats looking at the turkeys.

"Do you know what those goats are saying to each other about those turkeys?" he said. "They're saying, 'What kind of goats are *they?*' "

Another time, when Gale Donney, who is just a little girl, hollered, "*Snake! Snake!*" and everybody ran to where she was pointing and saw a worm, Ned Gage came up and said, "Stand back, that there snake's poison." He picked it up, and the girls screamed and ran. And then Ned Gage said, "To *eat*, I mean. So I'm not going to eat him." He dug a little hole with his finger in the soft earth and put the worm in the hole.

What skating we did on Macaroni Lane! What bike riding! What running! What rope jumping! What hopscotch playing!

I remembered California all the time.

In the middle of August in New York there was a hurricane, but it didn't come straight to New York, it went alongside of it. A day or two later there was a lot of rain. In some places the rain was so heavy the rivers overflowed, and a lot of cities had rushing water in the streets. There was a lot of damage, and I heard that a few people had drowned. I was sorry, but I was glad it hadn't been me. I'd hate to be drowned. *Ever.* I hate to think of *anybody* drowned. I don't understand being drowned. It's a terrible thing, and I wish it wouldn't happen. I wish it wouldn't happen to anything alive. It's an awful surprise. Whenever I think about it, I get scared.

In the first week of September, New York was a little cooler, but not much.

Mike McClatchey began to see people for the rest of the parts in the play. He saw hundreds of them, because that's the way it is. When actors and actresses hear that somebody is going to produce a play they go to his office. The play needed nine people, but Mike McClatchey said he saw more than nine *hundred.*

Mama Girl and I were at his office one morning when he was seeing people, and the whole front office was full of them—all kinds of them. It made me feel unhappy to see them. I don't know why, but it made me almost sick. They were all there together, some sitting, but most of them standing, and something was the matter. They wanted something. They wanted it badly, but they were almost sure they wouldn't get it, and that's no fun at all.

When I was little I was sick once, and I wanted something, only I didn't know what it was. My father sat by my bed and talked to me.

"I want," I said.

"I know, Twink."

"*What* do I want?"

"Everything, Twink."

"Can I have it?"

"Yes."

"When?"

"Just as soon as you're better."

"Right now?"

"In a little while."

"Tomorrow?"

"Tomorrow for sure."

"What will everything be?"

"*You*, Twink. You'll get yourself back the minute you're better. You'll forget you ever lost yourself. And that'll be everything."

"Is that all? Just me?"

"Yes, Twink. That's all there is."

"But I've *always* got me, Papa."

"Except now, because you're sick. Because when anybody's sick, he loses himself—but just for a little while. That's what sickness is. All of a sudden you're not there anymore, so of course you want—you want all kinds of things—everything—but what you really want is always yourself, because if you've got love, that's all there is—yourself and love, and I love you, Twink."

I guess that's the reason the people I saw at Mike McClatchey's made me feel sick. I could see they wanted something, and I couldn't give it to them. I hate to see somebody wanting something and not getting it. I felt ashamed when I saw them sitting and standing and just waiting, as if they were sick in bed with no father to sit beside them and hold their hands and let them know they are going to be all right pretty soon.

Wanting hurts. It hurts worse than anything. I'd rather go without than want. I've always got myself, anyhow, and plenty of time.

Helen Gomez sent us right on in to Mike's office, and Mama Girl said, "Oh, Mike, I wish you could give them *all* jobs."

"So do I," Mike said, "but of course I can't."

"Well, at least don't keep them *waiting*."

"They'd rather wait than have me go out and send them away. Kate wants to go to the country for a few days. She thinks it might be a good idea for you two to have a holiday, too. Where would you like to go until Sunday night? That gives you almost four full days. Monday we begin reading with the full cast—nine o'clock, here. Atlantic City? Connecticut? Where?"

"Paris," I said.

Mike McClatchey laughed and said, "Oh, no, not so far, please."

"Well," Mama Girl said, "I think I'd rather stay in New York and take in some plays."

"Better not," Mike said. "Please stay away from the theater. I've got my reasons. I don't want either of you to see anything. You'll get ideas, and I just don't want you to."

"Are you sure?" Mama Girl said.

"Absolutely. Kate's very happy about everything, and so am I, so stay away from the theater."

"Well," Mama Girl said. "All I *really* like is going for drives, but, of course, I don't have a car."

"I'll hire one," Mike said. "I'll have it at the hotel garage. Do you want a chauffeur?"

"I hadn't thought of it," Mama Girl said, "but it would be awfully restful just to sit in the back and go for long drives, and home every evening."

"A car with a chauffeur," Mike said. "Forget the play. Forget everything. Just have fun for four days."

"We'll go on a picnic every day."

"Good," Mike said. "Anything else?"

"Anything *else?*" Mama Girl laughed. "You mean there's *more?*"

We went back to where the people were waiting. Helen Gomez said, "Well? Where to?"

"Picnics," I said. "We're going on picnics every day."

"Come with us," Mama Girl said.

"Wouldn't I like to, though?" Helen said.

"Well, come—Sunday."

"Sundays are my busiest days. I don't just work in this office, you know. Have fun. See you Monday morning."

We went out of the office, and down to Fifth Avenue. We decided to walk home, window-shopping on the way. When we got back to the hotel the man at the desk said our car and chauffeur were waiting, and he said there was a picnic basket in our room. We went up to 2109, and there on the bureau was a big wicker picnic basket, full of food, the whole thing wrapped in green cellophane and tied with a green ribbon.

Mama Girl took the card out of the little envelope and read, "'To my Star, both of you. Love. Mike.'"

"Where shall we go?" Mama Girl said.

"Coney Island," I said.

"Oh, no."

"Oh, yes."

"But why, Frog?"

"Because you went there when you were a little girl. Because I didn't when I was a little girl. Because I've seen it in six or seven movies, and now I really want to see it. All right?"

Mama Girl laughed and said, "All right. I didn't expect the car to arrive until tomorrow, anyway, so we'll go to Coney Island."

"And have fun."

"And have fun."

"We'll ride everything."

"Well, almost everything. I just can't ride on some of those crazy things, but we'll go on a lot of them. We'll take five dollars each, and spend it, and come home."

Mama Girl gave me a five-dollar bill to put in my

handbag, she put another in her handbag, and then she put the rest of the money in the top drawer of the bureau.

She was excited and happy, and so was I. I couldn't wait to see that place.

"Just think," she said, "Miss Cranshaw is happy about our work."

"Why *wouldn't* she be?"

"Because she's not easy to please—because she expects perfection. And I'm glad she does, too. I've never worked so hard in my life."

"Call *that* work?"

"Of course I do."

"It's not work for *me.*"

"Of course not, because you're only nine years old, and everything is fun for you. You've got nothing to lose."

"Neither have you."

"Just everything," Mama Girl said.

"No."

"What do you mean—no?"

"You haven't got *anything* to lose, that's all."

"All right," Mama Girl said, "Miss Know-it-all."

"Take that back, or I'm not going."

"I take it back," Mama Girl said. "I wouldn't miss this trip to Coney Island for anything in the world, and I wouldn't have *you* miss it, either."

She telephoned the desk to ask the chauffeur to bring the car around to the front. We took the big picnic basket and went downstairs.

The car was a brand-new green Cadillac, and the chauffeur was a young Negro who told us his name was Leroy.

"Will you please drive us to Coney Island, Leroy?" Mama Girl said. "And please don't hurry, because we want to look at everything on the way."

"Yes, ma'am," Leroy said, and away we went.

We saw Greenwich Village, and the Brooklyn Bridge, and Brooklyn, and a lot of other places.

On the way Mama Girl loosened the ribbon of the picnic basket and gave it to me. Then she removed the green cellophane and folded it carefully and gave that to me, too. Then she examined what we had in the basket, and it was just about everything. We ate some sandwiches in the car as we were traveling. There was one Thermos with cold milk in it for me, and another with ginger ale in it for Mama Girl.

It was after four when we got to Coney Island. We were still there at seven o'clock, and we still had a dollar each to spend, so just for the fun of it we decided to go to the shooting gallery and spend twenty-five cents each and shoot at the tin ducks moving across the water. The man at the shooting gallery told us how to hold a rifle, how to aim, how to press the trigger, and then we took turns shooting.

Mama Girl shot at a duck and missed, and then I shot at one and missed, too. But by the time we had shot three times each we had learned how to do it and we began to hit the ducks.

It's a thrill to get a duck in the sight of the rifle, press the trigger before it's too late, and then see the tin duck fall. First the sound of the shot, then the sound of the bullet striking the tin duck, and then *plunk!*

We still had seventy-five cents each, but we decided to keep it in case we wanted to stop on the way home and buy something. We left Coney Island and went back to the Cadillac, and there was Leroy sitting behind the wheel reading a book.

We were on the Brooklyn Bridge when the lights of New York went on, and then we really saw a sight. There it was—New York, at night. We looked at each other, and then Mama Girl hugged me and I hugged her.

When Leroy let us out at the Pierre he asked Mama Girl if she'd like him to be ready very early in the morning, in case we wanted to go somewhere far. Mama Girl thought a moment, and then she said, "Not tomorrow, Leroy. Perhaps the day after. If you'll come at ten tomorrow morning, I think that'll be soon enough."

We went upstairs with our picnic basket and looked out our window. We laughed because summer lightning was flashing and making quick purple light, and we were there, and then we heard the clap of thunder, and we were in New York, and soft rain began to fall and we were all right, out of trouble, nobody sick, and good things to come.

Chapter 23

Poor Old Marriage

*T*he soft rain made New York and the night smell sweet. It made everybody in the world seem to be all right at last, like three-year-old Gale Donney when she used to stand in her nightgown on the lawn of her house on Macaroni Lane. She used to stand there early in the morning, and not look at anything. She used to be awake, because her eyes were open, but it seemed as if she were still dreaming, and still inside her dream. I used to see her from the window of my room. It seemed as if she was trying to remember something. The soft rain of New York made me remember her.

Mama Girl turned off the light. We stood in the dark at the window and watched and listened to the rain.

Then the telephone rang, and everything changed.

It was Gladys Dubarry, and from the way Mama Girl talked to her I knew Gladys was in trouble. They talked almost a whole hour.

"What's the matter?"

"She had a fight with her husband," Mama Girl said, "and he struck her. She wants to call the police. She says she didn't know she married a crazy man. She says he's threatened to kill her. She's afraid to stay in the same house with him. She wanted to come here to spend the night, but of course I told her she couldn't. I just don't know what to do for her. He's not the kind of man to strike his wife. He probably *shoved* her. She's hysterical and needs sedatives, she says, but she hasn't got any more and he won't give her any more because he says she doesn't need any—all she needs is a spanking. She wants me to take a taxi and go there."

"Are you?"

"Of course not. Marriage is something a woman works out alone—or *doesn't*. Besides, we're on holiday. All I want to do is soak in a tub and go to bed. How about you?"

"Me, too. I feel sorry for her, though."

"Well, don't you think I do, too? I've known her since we were both six or seven. She's always been impossible, of course, but she's really a good person inside."

"I know. I like her. If you want to go to her, go ahead. I won't be afraid. I'll just have a bath and go to sleep."

"No," Mama Girl said. "I want to try to be her friend, of course, but it would be a mistake to go to her at a time like this. It would be unfair to poor Hobart, and to her, too. It really isn't anything unusual at all. It happens to every husband and wife sooner or later. It's part of marriage, and marriage just isn't easy, that's all—for anybody. If you're both very poor, marriage is difficult. If you're both very rich, it's difficult. If one of you is rich and the other is poor, it's difficult."

"Why?"

"Because in a marriage one's a man and the other's a woman."

"Would it be easier if both were women?"

"That wouldn't be a marriage."

"Why not? Takes two to make a marriage. Well, two women."

"Two women can't have children."

"They can adopt them, can't they?"

"No, because children don't expect two mothers. They expect a father and a mother—their *own*. One mother is enough for children. Too much, sometimes. And I've got an idea that that's really what they're fighting about."

"*What* is?"

"Children."

"Do they *have* children?"

"No, that takes a little time, but all the same that's probably what they're really fighting about, although they probably think it's about something else. I'm sure he wants her to be a real woman and have a child, and she just can't be a real woman yet."

"She *looks* like a real woman."

"It's something inside that you can't see. It's a very difficult thing to be, too."

"*You* were a real woman when you were married, weren't you?"

"I wonder," Mama Girl said. "I had your brother, and then I had you, but I wonder. Even having children may not do it."

"I don't understand."

"Of course not. I'm thirty-three, and I'm just *beginning* to."

"What *is* a real woman?"

"In a marriage a real woman lives for her husband, and he lives for her, because living for each other means children and a family, and a family is the most important thing for men and women and boys and girls to have. A family is everything. It always has been. And families can happen only by marriages, but the trouble is, marriages are difficult—almost impossible."

"Why?"

"I don't know, but it has something to do with the way people think and live—what they believe, and what they want. Let's bathe and go to bed."

"All right, but you're not angry at *me*, are you?"

"No, of course not. Why should I be angry at you? I'm worried about poor Gladys and poor Hobart. It would be too bad if they did something silly."

"Maybe you ought to go to them."

"No, I *know* that's wrong."

We bathed and went to bed. I was almost asleep when Mama Girl sat up suddenly, grabbed the telephone, and gave the hotel operator Gladys's number. She waited a long time, but there was no answer. She got out of bed and lighted a Parliament. She asked the hotel operator to try the number again, but again there was no answer.

"What shall I do, Frog?"

"I don't know, Mama Girl."

She finished one cigarette and then lighted another. She got her clothes out of the closet and began to get dressed quickly, and then she took everything off again and put them away.

"No," she said. "It's none of my business. I'm here to work, that's all. I can't afford to think about anything but the play. The hardest work of all is just beginning. Gladys and Hobart will have to fight it out alone, the same as everybody else."

She shut off the light and got back in bed, but she wasn't relaxed at all. I wasn't, either. I couldn't be. I listened to the rain, but it didn't make me feel good anymore. I wanted to say something that would help Mama Girl to relax, but I couldn't think of anything.

"All I can say," Mama Girl said, "is Heaven help the married, especially Gladys and Hobart. They *need* help. They need a lot of it. They need more than any other husband and wife in the world."

"Yes," I said. "Heaven help them. But why do *they* need more?"

"Because she's still *got* to be Gladys Dubarry, rich girl, and as long as she goes on being Gladys Dubarry, rich girl, beautiful girl, society girl, gossip-column girl, and all the rest of it, there just *isn't* a marriage."

"What *is* there?"

"Twosies," Mama Girl said. "Him and her, killing each other in an endless and useless fight. Thank God I'm divorced. I had nine years of it, and that's enough. I gave him a bad time, but I didn't really mean to. He gave me a bad time, too, but I know *he* never meant to, either. We just couldn't help it."

"Is Hobart going to *kill* Gladys?"

"Of course not. She just *said* that. Are you asleep, Frog?"

"Almost, Mama Girl. Don't feel bad."

"I don't. *Really* I don't. Just a little sad—because I'm so glad it's all over, and I've still got you, and your father has still got you, and I've still got Pete, and he's still got his father, and you've both got us."

"And each other, too. You and my father have still got each other, too, haven't you?"

"Yes, I think so," Mama Girl said. "We're divorced, but we didn't even begin to be friends until we were."

Mama Girl didn't say anything for a long time and I almost fell asleep, and then she said, "All four of us have still got each other."

I don't know if she said anything more, because I fell asleep.

Coney Island kept going around in my head before I fell asleep. It was a place made for fun, bright and big and noisy. It was the best place of all to walk around in, look and listen, and ride things, and buy things—candied apples, and popcorn, and ice cream, and hot dogs, and soda pop. It was the best place of all.

Coney Island kept going around in my sleep, too, and I kept going around in Coney Island, and then all of a sudden there was my father with my brother, straight from Paris.

When the four of us saw each other we stopped and just looked, and then we all laughed and ran to each other and hugged and kissed and I said to myself, "I don't care how difficult it is for a man and a woman to be married, I don't care if they've got to get divorced so they won't kill each other, it's worth getting married and divorced when they meet at Coney Island, it's worth anything and everything when the man and the woman and their son and their daughter meet at Coney Island when they never expected to, after not seeing each other for a whole year. It's worth it, even if they only meet in a dream, like this one."

When I woke up I knew it was early in the morning. Everything is different when it's early in the morning. The things you hear from the streets are things the early-morning people do, like the trash and garbage men trying not to make too much noise with the trash cans, but you can always hear them just the same.

And the men who drive the big machines that sweep the streets with a brush that rolls like the brush in a floor sweeper. You hear the motor of the machine and the sound of the brush turning. They're down there early in the morning cleaning the city.

You hear the unloading of boxes with things to eat in

them for hotels and restaurants, too, and sometimes the voices of the working men.

"Hey, Louie. How about *this?*"

And then you hear laughter, and another voice says, "Very funny. You ought to be on television."

You hear the sound an automobile makes when it rolls along a quiet street.

You don't hear mockingbirds singing in eucalyptus trees, but that's all right, because the things you *do* hear are nice to hear, too.

Sometimes you hear an automobile horn, but if you want to hear a horn again, you've got to wait a long time. You don't hear whistles of any kind at all, but if you listen carefully, you hear somebody walking on the sidewalk.

It's fun to hear the early-morning sounds, because it's another day now, and you've forgotten everything you dreamed. The wonderful and happy things, the things that scare you, and the ones that make you so unhappy you know you must be sleeping because when you are awake *nothing* makes you *that* unhappy. All I remembered was Coney Island, and something, but what was it? We had *been* there, but what was it I couldn't remember that I was sure I would never forget when I woke up? I tried very hard to remember, but I couldn't, and then when I wasn't trying, I did.

It was my father and my brother from Paris standing there right in front of us. Just remembering what happened when we saw each other, even though I knew it hadn't really happened, made me happy all over again. I had *remembered* it, anyway, and it certainly *had* happened in my sleep, and that's something, too. That's not the same thing as really happening, but it's something.

Mama Girl smelled warm and deep inside of herself. I tried not to stir, so she wouldn't wake up, but when I turned very slowly, there she was with her eyes wide open, smiling.

"What you doing, Frog?"

"Listening."

"Me, too. Did you hear what he said to Louie?"

"Yes."

"Just hearing them made me proud."

"Of what?"

"Of being in New York, of being in a play, of having a chance to be just as real on the stage as they are in the street."

"Oh."

"Some people are so real, Frog, you don't even need to see them. It's in their voices. They're alive. They're men who do hard work, but they're very real, and sometimes you think they're the most famous people of all."

"Aren't they?"

"Oh, no. Nobody knows them."

"Who *is* famous?"

"Famous people are. Everybody knows *them.*"

"*Somebody* knows the people who aren't famous, too."

"Who?"

"Well, whoever they know," I said. "If Louie's got a wife, *she* knows him, and if Louie and his wife have got children, *the children* know them—their father and mother. And then there are other people who know them, too. I didn't know *you* were listening, too."

"I've been awake since six o'clock," Mama Girl said. "I woke up at six sharp—*without* a telephone buzz. It's almost seven now."

"Are you going back to sleep?"

"Oh, no. I'm too happy."

"I'm not going back, either."

"I thought we'd have breakfast up here, and just enjoy our freedom. All right?"

"Oh, yes."

"I'll ask room service to fix us a picnic lunch, and they can bring it up when they bring breakfast."

"We still have a lot of things in the basket. Let's eat *them* all up."

"All right. Where shall we go?"

"Somewhere *you'd* like to go."

"We'll drive across the George Washington Bridge, then, to Jersey, and drive through some of the towns over there."

"Which ones?"

"Well, Paterson, and Union City, and Rahway, and maybe six or seven others."

"Are they beautiful cities?"

"Oh, no."

"Then why do we want to see them?"

"Oh, they're part of my past, and I haven't seen them in a long time. We'll have fun looking at streets and places I used to know."

"What did *you* dream, Mama Girl?"

"I don't remember, but I know I dreamed *something.*"

"Were you at Coney Island, maybe?"

"Maybe, but I'm not sure."

"I was."

"Was it fun?"

"Better than when we were *really* there."

"Is that so?"

"Yes, and just try to guess who else was there."

"Who?"

"My father and my brother."

"Where was I?"

"With me, of course."

"How *were* they?"

"Just fine."

"How were we?"

"Just fine, too. We all stopped when we saw one an-other. We all laughed, and then we ran and hugged and kissed."

"What a nice dream. I hope it didn't end too quickly."

"It didn't end at all, because I didn't forget it, but at first I did. What *is* a dream, Mama Girl?"

"Oh, that's one I just *can't* answer, Frog. That's one everybody's been trying to answer ever since human beings *began* to dream."

"When *did* they begin?"

"I'm not sure, but I suppose it began when they wanted things to be different or better."

Mama Girl got out of bed and brought everything out of the picnic basket.

"Oh, yes," she said, "we've got plenty here for today. I'm going to have a very sensible breakfast, and I want you to, too. Prunes. Oatmeal. Boiled eggs. Toast. Hot cocoa."

"Ugh! Can't we have something else?"

"Prunes and oatmeal are very good for us."

"We haven't had them before. Why do we have to have them now?"

"Because we're going to Jersey, and that's what I used to eat when I was there. It'll be fun. This'll be our Jersey day. All right?"

"Sure, Mama Girl. I hate prunes and oatmeal, but I'll gobble them up."

"I hate them, too, but I'm sure they'll be delicious after twenty-five years."

"Why?"

"Because I'm happy now."

"Weren't you happy then?"

"Oh, no, Frog."

Mama Girl telephoned room service and ordered breakfast. She asked the order girl to have the waiter bring the morning papers with breakfast.

"I'm almost afraid to look at them," she said.

"Why?"

"I just hope poor Gladys and poor Hobart haven't got themselves splashed all over the front pages."

When breakfast came Mama Girl took the *Mirror* and turned the pages quickly, and then put it aside and sat down.

"Thank God," she said. "There's nothing in the *Mirror*, and if there's nothing in the *Mirror*, there's nothing in any of them. Well, let's eat our Jersey breakfast."

We started with the prunes, of course, and they weren't bad at all. They were kind of good, even. It was nice getting the stone away from the mushy part and tasting the stone a moment before putting it back in the spoon. We poured sugar and cream over the oatmeal, and it wasn't bad, either.

"Oh, how I hated them both," Mama Girl said, "but not any more. They're just food now. Do *you* hate them, Frog?"

"Oh, no. I'm not crazy about them, but I don't hate them, either."

It was a nice breakfast, and when we were all finished it wasn't even eight o'clock yet, and we had a whole happy new day ahead of us.

Chapter 24

Players, to Work

*T*hursday we went to Coney Island, Friday to Jersey, Saturday to Connecticut. Sunday we drove all around Manhattan, because tomorrow was Monday.

The holiday was fun. We talked and talked. About everything, I mean, and everything was always the play.

Monday morning the phone rang at six, and we got up and went to work. We walked in the Park, had breakfast in the Coffee Shop, went upstairs to 2109, and studied our parts. At eight o'clock Miss Cranshaw telephoned and asked us to walk with her to Mike's office, so we did.

We thought we were going to be the first to arrive, but we were the last, even though it was only half past eight and we weren't supposed to start work until nine.

Everybody was seated around the big table Mike McClatchey had moved out from the wall to the center of the room.

"I'm glad we're all here, and early," Mike said, "because I think it would be a good idea for us to hear the tape recording Oscar Bailey has made of the music. We'll begin to read immediately afterwards."

Mike nodded to Oscar, and Oscar said, "I've spoken to the composer on the telephone about the music and the instruments in the band, which are piano, violin, trumpet, drums and percussion, banjo, oboe, electric organ, xylophone, and various toy instruments. Some of the instruments were indicated by the composer, and some we agreed upon in our talk. We had planned to use the human voice, too, both male and female, in shouts more than in song, but I wasn't able to find the kind of voices I wanted. This is not quite the way the music will be at our first performance, but it *is* a beginning, and I think it is a pretty good one, all things considered."

Oscar started the tape recorder, and we began to hear the music played by musical instruments in a band, instead of on the piano alone. Oscar is a man who doesn't like to brag, I guess, because the music had been wonderful when he had played it on the piano, but now it was even more wonderful, and sometimes it was so funny it made you laugh out loud.

When the music ended, everybody applauded, and Mike McClatchey put his arm around Oscar and said, "Thanks, Oscar. I think it's the best music of its kind I've ever heard."

"What are we going to leave out?" Oscar said.

"We'll see," Mike said. "Now, to work."

Oscar began to go, and Mike said, "Oh, no, I want you to sit through this first reading, please. Immediately after the reading the cast can break for lunch while the rest of us discuss our—problems."

Mike pressed a button and Helen Gomez came in.

"Helen," he said, "no interruptions here until further notice, please. We may be two hours, we may be three."

Helen nodded and smiled and went out and shut the door behind her.

Mike introduced everybody quickly, and then he asked Emerson Tully to say a few words.

Emerson said, "This is a play. So far it's a play in manuscript. We are now going to turn it into a play on the stage. Our first performance before an audience in a theater will take place at the Forrest Theatre in Philadelphia two or three weeks from today or tomorrow, depending on the kind of luck we have, and other technical matters. Let's read it, then."

Everybody was seated, including a short heavy man named Joe Trapp who was the set and costume designer, and everybody had a copy of the play.

Emerson said, "I'll read the descriptions and business." After a moment—after looking at his watch—he began to read.

The time was half past nine.

It was my turn to read next. Everybody was very quiet, and I think I read better than I had ever read before, but of course I knew my lines by heart. If I hadn't, I wouldn't have been able to say them the way I did, because I read slowly.

The next to read was an old man, the grandfather of the little girl. He had a deep voice, and a nice way of speaking. After him it was the turn of a girl named Agnes Hogan.

After her it was Mama Girl's turn, and she read very well, but I knew she was a little scared, because I had heard her read the same lines much better many times.

Little by little the whole play was read.

For a minute nobody said anything, and then everybody began to speak at once, especially the ones who hadn't read the play before.

Mike said, "Thank you very much, ladies and gentlemen. If you'll be back here in an hour and a half, at two, we'll read it again."

Everybody got up to go, so Mama Girl and I did, too, but Mike said, "I want you to stay."

"I was hopeless," Mama Girl whispered to Mike. She looked very unhappy.

Mike just smiled at her.

When the rest of the cast was gone Mike said, "The time has come for blunt language—on the part of every one of us here. Emerson?"

Emerson Tully rubbed his chin, and then he said very softly, "I've got a lot of work to do, Mike."

"What kind of work?"

"Rewriting."

"I don't agree, but we'll talk about that later. What about the cast?"

"Some of them I liked very much—perhaps too much. But I think *all* of them are very good."

"Anybody *entirely* wrong?"

"No. I like them."

"Oscar?" Mike said.

"I'm a musician," Oscar said, "but I'll say *this*—I've never heard anything from the stage of a theater that I've enjoyed more."

"Is the music going to blend in all right?"

"I think so. I even think we can use it all—but you're the boss, Mike."

"I don't want to be the boss," Mike said. "Remember, everybody, now is the time to get this play going the way we believe it *ought* to go, so please speak up. Anything you didn't like, anything that seemed wrong, anything at all. What about their voices, as *voices*, Oscar?"

"Every voice is different, Mike, and I think every voice *should* be. Was that an accident?"

"Not quite," Mike said. "What about the different per-

sonal styles of speech—aren't they just a little too different? Musically?"

"No," Oscar said. "I like them that way."

"Any ideas, then?"

"Yes. When they read again, could they be standing? I
mean, I'm thinking of them as dancers."

"We'll come back to that in a minute. Kate?"

"Now, what do you *expect* me to say, Mike?"

"Exactly what's on your mind, and I know it's plenty.
Let's have it. *All* of us."

"Emerson's got a lot of hard work to do, but I don't
mean rewriting. I don't think he should change a word.
Now, Emerson, I've worked with a lot of playwrights, and
the first thing they think when words fall flat is that
something is the matter with the words, and sometimes
something *is*, but not this time. Your hard work is with
your people."

"Who don't you like, Kate?" Mike said.

"I don't dislike any of them. As a matter of fact, I think
you've done an excellent job of casting, but you must
understand that in New York we don't have a real theater,
we don't have real players, we have ambitious people, and
that's something else. Emerson's got to transform seven
nice, ambitious people into true players in a couple of
weeks."

"With *your* help," Mike said. "That shouldn't be impossible, should it?"

"I hope not," Kate said. "The little girl and her mother
are the play, of course, but unless the rest of the people
play their parts with daring and imagination and even
genius, there isn't likely to *be* a play."

"But you're not worried, are you?" Mike said.

"Of course I'm worried," Kate said. "If I weren't, I
wouldn't be here. I like Emerson's play. I think it's the

only play I've seen in years that deserves the time and
trouble it takes to get a play on the boards."

"All right, Kate," Mike said. "Joe?"

"I've got no fault to find," Joe Trapp said. "As for the
set, I see it made out of almost nothing—and light. Little
edges of things, and light. Straight light, and then possibly two or three colors, but not too strong. And of course
shadows. Single, double, triple, big and small—all kinds
of them, but not every minute of the play, just when
they're right. As for costumes, I've got a lot of ideas—a *lot*
of them, but the little girl should be barefoot most of the
time."

"Why?" Emerson and Mike said at the same time.

"I don't know just yet," Trapp said. He brought a big
handkerchief out of the pocket of his jacket and mopped
his face with it. "I've got good reasons, but I don't know
what they are just yet. Don't you think the little girl
should be barefoot, Kate?"

"I hadn't thought about it," Miss Cranshaw said, "but
now that you mention it, I believe I do."

"*Why*, though?" Mike said. "I kind of like the idea,
too, but Emerson hasn't mentioned it in the play, and I'd
like to know why you two like the idea."

"Well," Trapp said, "she's a dancer. Everything she
imagines happens like a dance. Her speech is like a dance.
But it's not ballet, it's childhood dancing. Barefoot—she
goes quick and silent."

"All right," Mike said. "We'll go back to that later."

Then he asked Mama Girl to say something. I was
afraid she was going to say she had read badly, but she
didn't.

She said, "Mike, I'm here to learn. I thought everybody
was just right, but what do I know?"

"Good enough," Mike said. "We'll get back to that

later, too. In fact, that may be our policy beginning tomorrow. Everybody is just right. I rather think everybody *is,* as a matter of fact. But this is the time to decide. Twink, how do *you* think it went?"

"Fine," I said.

"O.K.," Mike said.

He pressed a button and Helen Gomez came in.

"We'll have that food now, Helen, please," Mike said.

Helen pushed in a cart with food on it, and everybody took sandwiches and coffee, but nobody stopped talking.

When I was alone with Mama Girl at the window looking down at New York and the East River I said, "You were wonderful, Mama Girl."

"I wasn't relaxed," Mama Girl said. "I've got to find out how to be relaxed."

"Don't *care* so much," I said. "How can you be relaxed if you care so much?"

Marna Girl took my hand and whispered, "You're my pal, Frog. You're the best friend I have in the whole world. I'll be relaxed next time, you wait and see."

Everybody came back about half an hour ahead of time, because they were all so excited about the play, so Mike said, "Well, as long as we're all here, let's read it again, straight through."

"Standing," Oscar said.

So we took places and read it again. This time Mama Girl was relaxed, and everybody noticed how much better she was. The others were better, too.

It was almost five when we were finished. Mike asked everybody to stay and have coffee and get acquainted, so we all sat and talked.

Mike asked if we'd like to hear the music again, and we did, so Oscar turned the machine on again, but he said,

"Don't stop talking to listen, though. Go right ahead." So we talked and listened to the music at the same time.

When it was time to go the man who played the part of the little girl's grandfather said, "Mr. McClatchey, you've got a lovely play, and I'm proud to be in it."

"It's an honor to *have* you in it, Mr. Mungo," Mike said. "In the old days of the Palace, when I was a kid, you were my favorite song and dance man, but I never thought I'd have the honor of having you in one of my plays."

"Thank you," Mr. Mungo said softly. And then he smiled and nodded to everybody and went out.

Miss Cranshaw and Mike McClatchey looked at each other.

"He was the greatest," Kate said.

"He's not so bad right now," Mike said.

Mama Girl and I walked home, but when we got there we decided not to go up, we decided to keep walking.

We walked up Madison Avenue to Harlem, and it was a new place for me to walk in. We had driven through Harlem yesterday, and Leroy had told us about the different streets and places, but now we were right there on Lenox Avenue.

Harlem is full of children, tumbled out of the buildings into the streets. The little boys and girls play games on the sidewalks. They jump rope, and dance, and sing, and have fun. There were three boys who were eleven or twelve, and one of them had a banjo. He played and sang, and the other two sang and danced. They were the best in Harlem.

We went into a cafeteria up there and saw a lot of big baked apples, so we had one each, with cream, and then we went out and walked some more, but pretty soon it was night, so we got in a taxi.

On the way home Mama Girl said, "Well, Frog, we're on our way."

"Yes."

"I was scared all day, but I loved it just the same, and I'm not scared anymore."

We just sat, then, and looked at the people in the streets. I was scared, but I didn't say so, because it's contagious. I liked being in the play, I liked Mama Girl being in it, I liked my father's music being in it, but I was scared just the same.

And I didn't even know what I was scared of.

Chapter 25

The Preacher
in the Pulpit,
the Pitcher in the Box

*T*he whole week was work and sleep, and gone before I knew it. Saturday night I slept at Miss Cranshaw's while Mama Girl went to a party Mike McClatchey gave for some people called backers. Miss Cranshaw didn't go because she hates parties. She said backers are people with money to invest in plays.

I was allowed to stay up until almost ten. When I woke up, Miss Cranshaw was already up. We had breakfast together, and then she said I could run along to the Park.

"If you'd like to go to church with me, be back at half past ten and we'll go," she said.

I walked by 2109 but I didn't stop or knock, because I knew Mama Girl was in there fast asleep.

I had fun in the Park, and then I went back to Miss Cranshaw's. Mama Girl was there, and that was a big surprise.

"I just couldn't have fun at the party," she said, "so I came home early and went to bed."

"*You* couldn't have fun at a party?" I said.

"No, I couldn't," Mama Girl said, and then to Miss Cranshaw she said, "I hope Mike isn't upset with me for leaving early."

"Why should he be?" Miss Cranshaw said.

"Well, he'd asked all those people to the party, and I think he expected me to read for them."

"Not at all. I wouldn't *have* you read for them, and Mike knows it."

"Well, Emerson tried to describe the play, and Oscar sat at the piano and played some of the music. Does Mike *have* to have backers?"

"Yes, he does. Ordinarily, he would have given the party long before he had gone into production, but I think I know why he gave it afterwards this time."

"Why?"

"Because unless he had already gone into production, they would have been afraid to put money into the play. That's the kind of play it is."

"Suppose they *don't* put money in it?"

"The play won't be produced."

"Oh, no!" Mama Girl said. "Now I *am* worried. Hasn't Mike got enough money to produce it without backers?"

"I'm afraid not," Miss Cranshaw said. "But don't worry, they'll put their money into the play all right."

"But suppose they *don't?*"

"That's the theater, and the part I've *always* hated."

"But what about all your hard work? What about Emerson's, and Mike's, and mine, and Frog's, and everybody's?"

"In the theater," Miss Cranshaw said, "we always believe a play *will* be produced—in spite of everything."

"I'm worried," Mama Girl said. "I didn't like the looks of those people. I'm sure they are going to think twice before they put money into the play."

"Well, Twink and I are going to church. Perhaps you'd better come along, too."

"I think I'd better, too. I'll pray for the backers to put money into the play."

"Forget the backers," Miss Cranshaw said. "Just come and sit and look. Just sit and study the theater. You'll see *real* theater at the church."

"I'm worried," Mama Girl said.

"Don't be," Miss Cranshaw said. "We have *got* to believe the play will be adequately backed, and effectively produced and performed. In the meantime, we must go about our business. Now, settle this matter in your heart. It's silly to worry."

"All right," Mama Girl said. "I won't worry anymore."

We walked down Fifth Avenue to Fifty-seventh, up Fifty-seventh to Broadway, down Broadway, and there I saw the church. We went in and watched the play in there. It was a soft play, very gentle, and a little sad—but sad in a way that didn't hurt. The whole inside of the church was the stage, and it was big. It was so big nobody in there could be bigger than he ought to be, or bigger than he really is. Everybody there was in the play, but the play was much bigger than anybody. It was even bigger than everybody put together. The play wasn't even the things the people said or did. It was the way the things there made everybody think and feel and remember, and these things were all soft and kind and gentle—not angry and swift and hard and loud. I felt at home in there. I liked being in there. There are a lot of famous actors in the theater, but in the church it's different. There isn't *any* actor. It's *all* the play—made out of peace and sorrow, and love and gladness—but no pride. Nobody *needs* to feel proud in a church.

We were there a long time, but I liked it. I liked every

minute of it, and I think Mama Girl did, too. She became relaxed and sad. I guess that's the word for it, but it wasn't *sad* sad, it was another sad. I don't think it was glad sad, either, but it was some kind of sad. A kind of sad that's better than any kind of glad, I guess. Nobody can be sad that way for very long, I guess. Just an hour or two once in a while—when you go to church. The minute you leave there you go back to feeling the way you always do.

When it was all over, Miss Cranshaw said, "Let's just sit and watch." So we sat and watched the people leave the church, and pretty soon the whole place was empty. Then Miss Cranshaw got up, and we went out to the aisle, but instead of going out to Broadway we went down the aisle to the front of the church, and we stood there and looked. Then we turned around and walked up the aisle, and Miss Cranshaw looked up to the top of the inside of the church, so I did, too—and there's a lot of high space in there. Beautiful space, surrounded by beautiful walls and ceilings and windows. When we were back on Broadway a few people were still standing on the steps of the church, in the sunlight, as if they didn't want to hurry away from that place.

We hailed a taxi and got in and Miss Cranshaw said, "To the Polo Grounds, please, and drive like mad or we'll miss the first pitch."

The driver turned around and smiled, and then he began to drive, but he didn't drive like mad. He drove swiftly but carefully.

"Well," Miss Cranshaw said, "how did you like it?"

"I loved it," Mama Girl said. "Let's go next Sunday, too. From now on, Frog, let's go every Sunday, wherever we are."

"Aren't we going to be here?"

"Well, we open in Philadelphia in eight or nine days," Miss Cranshaw said.

"We *will* open, won't we?" Mama Girl said.

"You're still worried," Miss Cranshaw said.

"Aren't *you?*" Mama Girl said.

"Of course I am. This is the first time I've been to church in almost a year. Mike doesn't show his own anxiety, but I've sensed for days that he's having money trouble. And this is one play I want to see on the boards—in New York. We've just got to bring the play in, and I'm terrified we won't be able to."

"Well, that's more like it," Mama Girl said. She even laughed a little. "I actually believed you *weren't* worried, and I couldn't understand it. I thought there must be something the matter with me. But why didn't you go to Mike's party and help?"

"Because I'm no help at all," Miss Cranshaw said. "If anything, I antagonize everybody who might otherwise be likely to put money in the play. Mike knows that, and he was relieved when I said I couldn't make it. I'm just no good at all in that department. From what you've told me about the party, I'd say Mike will manage all right. And, of course, Emerson has a warm and friendly quality with anybody he meets, as most young writers do. As they get older, though, they lose it. I enjoyed being at church very much, didn't you, Twink?"

"Oh, yes," I said, "but I can't wait to get to the ball game, too."

"Driver!" Miss Cranshaw called out. "Faster, please."

The driver turned around, and smiled again.

"From church to the ball game," he said. "Pretty good."

"Just about perfect for a Sunday, isn't it?" Miss Cranshaw said.

"*I'd* say so," the driver said.

He drove nice and steady, and we made it. We were in our seats at least a minute before the first pitch, and then

there it was—*another* play. A play something like the one
at the church, but right out in the sunshine, and full of
excitement and noise, all of us sitting on the edge of our
seats, watching and waiting, and shouting. It was a beautiful play, and I forgot all about the play at the church. I
even liked the baseball play better than the church one. It
was livelier and more fun, and you didn't need to bother
about feeling sad or glad or anything else. All you did was
watch and shout with happiness or anger. I was for the
Giants, and Miss Cranshaw was for the Dodgers.

Mama Girl wasn't for or against anybody. She didn't even
understand the game, a girl thirty-three years old. I learned
all about the game from my brother Peter Bolivia Agriculture. Miss Cranshaw explained the game to Mama Girl,
and I helped, but no matter how much we explained
Mama Girl just didn't understand. She pretended to, but
we knew she didn't, because how could she when she
thought it was awful when a pitcher struck out a batter?
Any pitcher. Any batter. She didn't understand that a
thing like that is a very great achievement for a pitcher,
even if it's not so good for the batter. And that's why
baseball's always exciting. One man's success is another
man's failure, and everybody is always trying.

The Dodgers won the game, but they didn't do it until
the top of the ninth. Miss Cranshaw was very happy, but I
was, too. The Giants are my team all right, but mainly
baseball is my game.

It was the best game I ever saw, but I kept wishing all
the time that my brother Pete were with me, and my
father beside my mother, even if they *are* divorced.

On our way home after the ball game Miss Cranshaw
said, "Look here, let's make a day of it, for tomorrow we
die of anxiety. What do you say we take in a movie?"

It was an Italian one called *Side Street*, and even though

I couldn't understand a word they were saying, or read the words in English on the screen fast enough, I loved it, because it was all about poor people and their troubles, especially a father who had a thin face and big tired eyes.

Well, he had a lot of trouble.

First, they put him in the Italian Army, or in something like the army, I'm not sure what it was. He had a uniform, and looked sad in it.

One day he got lost and asked an Italian which way to go to avoid the Germans or somebody—another army—and the other Italian told him to go down the steps and around to the right, but when he did, the Germans were waiting and captured him. They took him far away to a prison and kept him there for a long time.

While he was gone his wife made love to another Italian, his daughter made love to an American soldier who went away and left her with a little boy, and everybody was poor and hungry.

It was beautiful, every bit of it, and I'll never forget the father, especially when he came home and found everything changed, sadder than ever. He went back to his work the same as ever, and had a lot of trouble with his wife, his daughter, and his son, who was now a young man. One day his son shouted at him because the son's bread was gone, and the son said his father had eaten it. I don't remember if he *had*, but I'll never forget that father, and his family. They were my friends, every one of them, and I loved them.

After the movie we walked home. We stopped at the Automat on Fifty-ninth Street, not far from the Pierre, and had supper there.

The whole day was a lot of fun, but I knew Mama Girl was worried, and so was Miss Cranshaw.

Chapter 26

Money

*M*onday morning we were all at Mike McClatchey's before nine, ready to go back to work. Mr. Trapp was showing Mike a model of the set for the play. It was one place that could be made into six or seven places by turning something around. Emerson Tully was watching the way the model worked, and Oscar Bailey, too. But nobody seemed happy about it, or about anything, so I knew something was wrong. Mr. Trapp marked the floor of Mike's office so that it would be like the set for the beginning of the play.

Then we went to work, with Emerson telling us where to stand and what to do as we said our lines. We worked that way until half past twelve, and then everybody in the cast except Mama Girl and me went to lunch.

Kate Cranshaw looked at Mike and said, "All right, Mike. Let's have it."

"We didn't do too well with the backers, I'm afraid," Mike said.

"What *are* the figures?" Miss Cranshaw said.

"We need about seventy-five thousand dollars," Mike said. "I've put everything I've got in—about seventeen thousand. I've got ten more from as many backers, and pledges for three or four more, but that's all. I've been counting on one or two backers putting in twenty or thirty thousand—for a group of investors, that is—but they haven't, and from the looks of things they're not *going* to."

"What are your plans?"

"We're going to open in Philadelphia—*that's* for sure."

"And then?"

"We'll see. If the audience likes the play—if the reviews are good—we're not going to have any trouble raising any amount we care to name."

"If they're bad?"

"I don't know," Mike said. "I've never seen backers so reluctant to gamble. The party was a flop."

"My fault, too," Emerson Tully said.

"Not at all," Mike said.

"I don't know how to talk to people like that," Emerson said. "I know I said the wrong things. I said I thought the play was a good play, but I just didn't know if it would be a hit. That was a mistake, Mike. Everybody *heard* me say it, too. I thought they would understand that nobody knows if *any* play is going to be a hit, but I guess it scared them. I'm sorry. Maybe you'd better try again, and I'll stay away."

"No," Mike said. "I invited everybody, and they were there. We've just got to plan for Philadelphia. The skeptics will be there opening night, of course, but if it goes well, they'll come forward."

We had lunch in the office, and when the cast came back we rehearsed some more. Everybody knew something was the matter, but they worked hard just the same. When we broke up for the day everybody said good-by kind of softly, not the way it used to be.

When Mama Girl and I got to the Pierre, there were some letters for us—one for me from my father, and in the

same envelope one from Peter Bolivia Agriculture. My
father said Oscar Bailey had sent him the tape recording of
the music, but he had had to look all over for a machine
to play it on. At last he'd found a machine and he'd
listened to the music, and it was pretty good, but he had
written a long letter to Oscar telling him how it could be
improved. My brother said he had taught some Paris boys
how to play baseball, and one of them, a boy named Jack,
pitched real good. I decided to write to both of them right
away. I wanted to tell my brother I saw a real good
National League game—Dodgers 2, Giants 1. And I wanted
to tell my father I saw him in Coney Island. Did *he* see me
there?

The letter for Mama Girl was in a very big envelope
made out of paper that felt like silk and was colored light
blue. On the envelope were great big initials in script—*G.D.*

"Listen to this," Mama Girl said. " 'For old times' sake,
for the beautiful past, telephone me the minute you get
this. It's a matter of life and death, but I can never again
humiliate myself by phoning you, because you have made
it quite clear that you loathe my doing so. Glad.' "

"Who's Glad?"

"*Gladys,* of course," Mama Girl said. "It's what I used
to call her when we were both very little. She's got her
nerve sending me such an insulting note."

"Call her."

"Never. I'm mad at her for *sure,* now."

"No, call her.

"Why should I?"

"It's a matter of life and death."

"It's a matter of *nothing*—the way it always is with her.
Can I read your letters?"

"Sure," I said. "They both send their love, of course."

We traded letters, and I read the one from Gladys

Dubarry. Her handwriting is big, all over a big folded square of fine blue paper, with a thin red line around it. A few words all over the first page, a few all over the second, and her name all over the back.

The telephone rang and Mama Girl talked to Miss Cranshaw, and then she said, "I've got to go down the hall to Miss Cranshaw's—I'll only be a minute."

When she was gone I found some hotel paper and began to write a letter to my father, but I write slowly and I wanted to say so much I couldn't say anything—almost. *My dear father,* I wrote. *I love you.* And then I stopped.

I went to the telephone and lifted the receiver, but I don't think I knew what I was going to do. I think I really wanted to call my father and talk to him, but I knew I shouldn't do that, and when the operator came on the line I couldn't think of any number except Gladys Dubarry's, so I gave her that number.

The telephone rang once and then it was answered. People who are *waiting* for the telephone to ring do that. I've seen Mama Girl do it, but most of the time she lets it ring a few times. I didn't recognize the voice. It seemed old and tired.

"Gladys?"

"Yes. Is that you, Frog?"

"Yes, Gladys."

"I'm so glad you called, because I've got to talk to your mother."

I didn't know what to say, so I said, "She had to go down the hall a minute. She just got your letter."

"Down the hall?" Gladys said. "You've got a bath in your own room, haven't you?" She sounded like herself now, and that made me feel much better.

"Oh, yes," I said. "She had to visit Miss Cranshaw."

"Who?"

"Kate Cranshaw. The greatest dramatic coach in the world. She's our teacher. She knows everything about acting, and everything else. I love her."

"You love everybody."

"I don't, either. I love a few. I *like* many. I don't know the rest."

"Who do you hate?"

"Nobody."

"I hate everybody," Gladys said.

"You do *not.*"

"Everybody but *you,* Frog. Most of all I hate *me.*"

"You do *not.*"

"I do."

"Why?"

"I just do. I think I *always* have. I'm sick and tired of me, and I don't know what to do."

"Why don't you drink a Coke?"

"I just did. It didn't do any good."

"Why don't you go to church, then?"

"On *Monday?* I didn't go Sunday."

"Can't you go on Monday?"

"What for? Nobody's there."

"The church is."

"So what?"

"Well, if you go, *you'll* be there, and you can say a prayer, and stop hating everybody."

"I don't want to stop. I *like* hating everybody. I just don't like hating *me.* Besides, I'm no good at church. I get the giggles."

"You *do?* I haven't had the giggles at church since I was very little. What *is* the matter, Gladys?"

"Ho. Ever since we had that fight, he won't talk to me."

"Do you *want* him to talk to you?"

"Of course I do. We're married."

"Well, why don't *you* talk to him?"

"I *couldn't* do that. It's too humiliating."

"Anything else?"

"Isn't that enough? I hate everybody, and Ho won't talk to me."

"Have you got a son yet?"

"I haven't been *married* a month yet."

"Well, a daughter, then?"

"You can't have a son *or* a daughter in one month."

"Yes, you can, if you *want* to. You *don't* want to."

"Even if you *want* to, you *can't*—in a month."

"Surprise him. He'll be thrilled."

"I'll *bet* he will."

"Just take him a son by the hand and everything will be all right again."

"Again? By the hand? Frog, I don't believe you understand *anything*."

"Yes, I do. I've seen them do it. They hold the hand of a small boy or girl who can barely walk and they take the child to the father, and he gets very happy and picks up the child and they hug and kiss."

"*Who* hugs and kisses?"

"The father and the child, and then the mother, too."

"Where did you see *that* happen? In a movie?"

"No, I saw it happen in my own house. I was the child. You do that, too, and Ho will hug and kiss the child, and *you*, too."

"Now, Frog," Gladys said. "Let me speak to your mother, please."

"She's not here."

"Well, when she gets back, please be sure she calls me, will you?"

"All right. Good-by, Gladys."

"Good-by, Frog."

I went back to my letter to my father and I wrote, *I miss you. I want to come to Paris.* But I knew that was wrong, so I scratched it out. The letter looked bad now, so I squashed it and threw it in the wastepaper basket. Then I began to write a letter to Mama Girl, because she was gone, too.

Phone Gladys. Love. Frog.

I put the letter on her pillow. That's where she likes to receive her mail. I looked around 2109, then out the window, then I saw the letter on the pillow and read it. It was short. I read it again. Then I dropped it into the wastepaper basket, too.

I wrote a new one. *Gone.* I put it on the pillow, and I got ready to hide the minute I heard the key in the door. I was ready for a long time, but I didn't hear anything, and I forgot all about hiding when Mama Girl came back.

She went straight to the letter and read it.

" 'Gone'?" she said. "What's that mean?"

"Just a little letter," I said.

She dropped it into the basket, and then she saw the others in there. She picked them out, and read them to herself.

Then she read one of them out loud: " 'My dear father. I love you. I miss you. I want to come to Paris.' "

She didn't even look at me when she said, "Do you *really* want to go to Paris?"

"Oh, no, Mama Girl," I said, because I didn't want her to get worried, but of course I've *always* wanted to go to Paris. Not just to *be* in Paris, but to see my father and my brother.

"Why did you write this, then?"

"I didn't know what else to write."

" 'Phone Gladys,' " she read.

"Why don't you?" I said.

"Because I can't be bothered. I've got too much to worry about already. You. Me. The play."

"What's the matter, Mama Girl?"

"Miss Cranshaw got an idea for me in the second act, so I went there, and we worked on it. Then we talked about the play and the money, and I'm terribly discouraged. It would be awful if the play closed in Philadelphia."

We were talking when somebody knocked on the door very loudly. This made Mama Girl jump, and she was very angry when she opened the door.

It was Gladys Dubarry.

"How dare you knock at my door that way?" Mama Girl said.

"Well!" Gladys said. "There's a friendly welcome if I ever heard one."

"Oh, what do you want?"

Sometimes Mama Girl can be the rudest person in the whole world. When she is, I get mad at her. I get so mad I say to myself, "She's not my mother. My mother would never talk that way. She's somebody else. I was stolen from my mother when I was very little. This woman— whoever she is—stole me. She's a total stranger. I don't ever want to see her again. I want to find my real mother." But after a moment—sometimes even before I've stopped being mad—I don't believe she stole me at all. I believe she *is* my real mother, and I wish she wouldn't be so rude.

"I wish you wouldn't be so rude," I said.

"What do you expect me to be when somebody knocks at my door as if I were a criminal?"

"I didn't mean to frighten you," Gladys said, "but when I got out of the elevator a man who had asked for the *twenty-fifth* floor got out, too, and I got frightened. I *ran* here—and thank you for opening the door so quickly. He may be out in the hall right now."

"You and your lovers!" Mama Girl said. She swung the door open, and went out into the hall. "All right, Miss Sexually Irresistible of 1955, come out here and see for yourself."

"Don't talk to me in that horrible tone of voice, please," Gladys said.

"Come on out," Mama Girl said.

"Oh, come on back in and stop being vicious," Gladys said.

"Well, if you won't come out," Mama Girl said, "you can have the whole place to yourself."

She waited a moment, and then she turned and walked away.

"Mama Girl!" I said. But she didn't come back, and I felt *very* mad at her.

"Oh, Frog," Gladys said, "I'm so sorry. I'm so ashamed. But there *was* a man following me. Please let me shut the door."

Gladys shut the door and stood there a moment, listening. When she turned around her mouth was trembling and I felt very sorry for her.

"What's *happened* to your mother, Frog? She and I have had fights before, but I've *never* seen her—*crazy*. What's the matter with her?"

"She's worried about the play."

"What's the matter with the play?"

But now Gladys was crying, just as if she were a little girl instead of a grown woman, a very rich woman, a married woman, the wife of a doctor, Hobart Tuppence.

"Oh, Gladys," I said, "please stop crying."

"I can't help it," Gladys said. "Everybody hates me."

"I don't hate you."

"Everybody *except* you, Frog. And thank you very much for being my only true friend. I thought your mother was

my only true friend, but that was long ago. Thank God
your mother *had* you. If I have a son, and he's worthy of
you, I'd like you to be his wife."

"O.K.," I said. "When are you going to get him?"

"That's what I came to talk to your mother about, but
you saw how *she* treated me."

"She didn't *mean* to," I said. "She's upset. She's terribly
worried."

"About *what?* What has she got to be worried about?
She got married when she was just a little girl. She had a
wonderful husband, who adored her. A great composer,
not a doctor, not a man with pills in his pockets. She had
a handsome son. She had a lovely daughter. She got
divorced when she was still a beautiful young woman.
What has *she* got to be worried about?"

"Her big chance."

"Her big chance! She missed her big chance a long time
ago. How she ever got your father to marry her in the first
place is something I'll never be able to understand."

"You take that back, Gladys Dubarry!"

"All right, Frog. I'm sorry. I take it back. Do you
forgive me?"

"Yes, but why are grown-ups all so mean?"

"I don't know, but it's something terrible. Here I am
about to become a mother, and my husband won't even
talk to me. I came to ask your mother to go to him and
tell him."

"Tell him what?"

"I'm pregnant."

"What?"

"I'm going to become a mother."

"Since when?"

"Since the night I was married, but I didn't find out
until about a week ago. I wasn't sure, of course. Some-

times there are false alarms, so I waited, but it *wasn't* a false alarm. I went to a doctor and he told me."

"Does Ho know?"

"Of course not. We're not speaking. In a whole month we've been a husband and a wife just once, and we've been fighting ever since. I wasn't thinking of becoming a mother at all. You're the only person I've told. I came to tell your mother, but, no, she wouldn't even let me say hello. I'm worried, Frog. I don't know what to do."

"When will you be a mother?"

"Well, if everything goes according to schedule, sometime next April or May."

"Can't you hurry up?"

"No, I can't. I'm not sure I want it to happen at all."

"You're not sure you want to have a son or a daughter?"

"No, I'm not. My husband doesn't love me."

"Oh, yes, he does. He loves you very much."

"Does he *really*, Frog?"

"Yes, and *you* know he does, too."

"Then why won't he talk to me?"

"Because he wants you to be different now that you're his wife."

"How?"

"He wants you to be his wife."

"I *am* his wife."

"Really."

"Well, if I'm not his wife really, then I don't know how—really. I don't even know if I *want* to be a wife that way."

"You've *got* to."

"Why?"

"For your son—or daughter."

"Yes," Gladys said. "I've got to find out how. Well, isn't she *ever* coming back?"

"She's gone to Miss Cranshaw's, I think."

"Will you call her and tell her I'm sorry and ask her to please come back?"

"*You* call her."

"I *couldn't*, Frog. I've been so humiliated."

"No, you haven't. Just call her."

Gladys asked the operator to ring Miss Cranshaw's phone, but Mama Girl wasn't there. Miss Cranshaw asked us to visit her for tea.

"Well," I said, "all right, but *now* I'm worried about my mother. We'd better leave a note letting her know where we are."

Gladys wrote a note and left it on Mama Girl's pillow, and then I took her to Miss Cranshaw's.

"I've heard so much about you," Gladys said.

"But where's your mother, Twink?" Miss Cranshaw said.

"Downstairs," I said. "She's having a cup of coffee, because she's so worried about the play."

"We *all* are," Miss Cranshaw said to Gladys.

"Isn't it a good play?" Gladys said.

"It's a wonderful play. We're having trouble raising money to bring it to New York. We've got enough for the tryout in Philadelphia, but that's all."

Miss Cranshaw poured tea for all of us and we began to drink tea and eat cakes and cookies, but I just couldn't enjoy anything, not even the rum cake.

"What's the matter with you, Twink?" Miss Cranshaw said.

"I think I want to go to 2109 and take a nap."

"Really?"

"Yes."

"Do you have your key?"

"Yes."

"Well, all right, then. We'll both be here if you want us, won't we, Mrs. Tuppence?"

"Yes, I'd like to visit for a while if I may."

"Oh, come now," Miss Cranshaw said. "I'm delighted to have you."

"Really?" Gladys said. She was thrilled.

I went to 2109 and stretched out on the bed. I wished Mama Girl and I were home on Macaroni Lane. I wished I was in Paris with my father and my brother. I wished all four of us were in Paris. I wished all four of us were in the house on Macaroni Lane. I wished there were five of us instead of four. I wished there were six, then seven, then eight. I needed a little brother and a little sister, and then another little brother, and another little sister. I wished grownups weren't always in so much trouble.

I wished I didn't hate being in the play. I hated it. Sometimes I didn't hate it very much. Sometimes I almost liked it, but sometimes I hated it more than anything in the world. I had never wanted to be in a play. I wished I had never talked on the telephone to Mike McClatchey, because if I hadn't he wouldn't have heard my voice, and that was why I was in the play. I wished my voice would change. My mother's voice changed all the time. Sometimes it was full of love, but sometimes it wasn't. Sometimes it was alive and full of laughter, but sometimes it was tired and full of anger. I wished I didn't have a voice at all. I had never wanted to learn how to say and do things on purpose, on a stage, in front of people. I only wanted my father and my mother and my brother and my friends.

I couldn't fall asleep, and I couldn't feel glad about being in the play. Mama Girl had kept all of the newspaper stories with photographs of her and me, but I just couldn't feel glad about any of them. What would happen if I got up and went down to the Coffee Shop and said, "Mama Girl, I don't want to be in the play?" Could I do that?

No, of course not, so I thought I'd better try hard to be glad about it.

I tried and tried, but I just couldn't be. After a while, though, if I didn't feel glad, at least I didn't feel bad, either.

I got up and left 2109 and went to the elevators. I pressed the button and after a while an elevator stopped and I got in. I went to the Coffee Shop, and sure enough, Mama Girl was in a booth drinking coffee and smoking a Parliament. I went and sat across from her. I smiled and she smiled, and then she reached across the table and held my hand.

"I'm so ashamed," she said. "I don't know what's happened to us. Would you like something?"

"No."

"Please. A dish of ice cream?"

"All right."

Mama Girl called the waitress—Rosie was off duty—and she brought me a dish of ice cream.

Then, instead of going upstairs, we took a walk in the streets. When we got back it was night and we were tired. We went straight to bed, and I fell asleep.

The next day we felt a lot better, and we worked very hard.

Chapter 27

Oh You Philadelphia

Saturday we checked out of 2109, and went on a train to Philadelphia, to the Benjamin Franklin Hotel. Everybody in the play was at that hotel.

Sunday morning we went to the Forrest Theatre and rehearsed on the stage. Mr. Trapp's set was there on the stage. It wasn't quite in working order, but we rehearsed just the same, while the men put the set together, and made it work.

We worked all day and some of the night. We didn't get a chance to go to church, or to a ball game, we just stayed in the theater. We had lunch brought in, and then supper, too. Emerson Tully worked harder than anybody. Oscar Bailey rehearsed his musicians in another part of the theater until late in the afternoon, and then we started from the beginning, with the music. The costumes would be ready tomorrow morning, and tomorrow night we would give the first performance of the play in front of an audience.

Everybody was excited, but at the same time scared, too—but most of all happy.

I was happy, too. That's what happens when you're in a play. Everything is mixed up. Everybody's worried, but when the time comes to give the first performance everybody feels happy, too.

Monday morning there were six cleaning women in the theater, making it fresh and clean for the first performance. The orchestra was in the pit, and the set was in perfect working order. We put on our costumes, and Emerson and Mike and Joe Trapp studied us, and Joe made a few quick changes in some of our costumes, and then Emerson said, "All right, everybody—straight through, as if it were a performance in front of an audience."

We did the play.

Emerson Tully jumped up on the stage, and he said, "Thank you, ladies and gentlemen. Now let's rehearse curtain calls."

We did that about five minutes, and then Emerson and Mike and Miss Cranshaw had a talk, and after the talk Emerson said, "We've decided not to rehearse anymore. Everybody please go home and relax—and please feel confident, will you? The play went better than any of us expected it to. Until tonight, then, and good luck to all of you."

Mama Girl and I went out into the sunlight of the early afternoon.

We walked to the hotel and went up and tried to rest. Pretty soon Mama Girl fell asleep, lying on top of one of the beds, and then I fell asleep, too.

We were backstage in our dressing room at half past seven. It was a very exciting time. We put on our costumes, and Mama Girl put on my make-up, and then her own. We heard the overture, and then Mike McClatchey came and said, "This is it. Good luck."

Mama Girl and I went out and stood in the wings. Pretty soon it was time for me to go onstage, so I did. I felt awfully funny, because I knew the whole auditorium was full of people who would start watching me as soon as the curtain went up. They would see everything I did. They would hear everything I said.

I wished I was in Paris, and then the curtain went up, and the play began. I did everything I had learned to do, as if it was somebody else doing it, while I myself thought about other things, about being in Paris with my father, and about happy times on Macaroni Lane with Mama Girl, and other things.

The whole play was over before I knew it.

The curtain came down, and then for a moment everything was still. Everybody in the play ran onstage while the curtain was down, and we stood in line, the way Emerson had rehearsed us. The curtain went up, and then we heard applause. We bowed together, and the curtain came down. We heard applause again, and the curtain went up. We bowed again, and it came down again. Now five of the people in the cast went away quickly, leaving Mr. Mungo, Mrs. Cole, Mama Girl, and me. The curtain went up and the four of us bowed. The curtain came down, and now Mr. Mungo and Mrs. Cole went away, and Mama Girl and I were supposed to take a bow, but there wasn't very much applause. We waited for the curtain to go up once more, but it didn't, so we turned away and went to our dressing room. On the way I could hear Mama Girl whispering to herself, "Oh, hell!"

When we got to the dressing room she poured herself a drink of whiskey out of a bottle I didn't even know she had, and she drank it down in one gulp. She lighted a Parliament, and inhaled deeply. She just stood in front of the mirror looking at herself.

"I stink," she said.

"That's all right, Mama Girl. I do, too. *Everybody* does."

She sat down then.

"I don't belong in the play," she said. "I don't belong in *any* play."

"I don't, either."

"Well, there it is," she said. "My big chance."

"Let's go to Paris," I said.

"We *can't* go to Paris," Mama Girl said. "We can't go anywhere. We've got to stay in Philadelphia. We've got to do the play for people who don't like us."

"Well, we don't like them, either, then."

Mama Girl poured another drink and gulped it down.

"I'm sorry, Frog," she said. "I had no right to drag you into this."

"I don't care, Mama Girl."

"If your father were here tonight, he'd be very angry at me."

"He read the play. He said I could be in it."

"Sure he did, because he knew that if you weren't, I couldn't be, either. He did it for me."

"He wrote the music for the play."

"He did that for me, too. I feel absolutely disgraced. I'm afraid to face anybody." She poured one more drink and gulped it down, and then she said, "Well, I guess I'm just not cut out to be an actress, that's all. I guess I'm just not somebody who can be famous, that's all. God knows, I tried. I worked. I worked very hard—night and day. Six long weeks I've lived nothing but this play, and my part. For what? To make a public fool of myself, that's all."

There was a very soft knock on the door, and Mama Girl put the bottle away. She looked at herself in the mirror, and then something happened to her face. She stopped looking mad.

She opened the door, and it was Gladys Dubarry, holding a big bunch of red roses.

"I knocked as softly as I could," Gladys said. "Can I come in?"

"Oh, Gladys!" Mama Girl said. "I had no idea you were in Philadelphia. Please come in."

Gladys stepped into the small room. She held the roses out to Mama Girl. They embraced quickly, and then Gladys gave me a hug, and the three of us just stood there. We didn't say anything, and then at last Gladys said, "I don't know what to say."

"Don't say anything," Mama Girl said. "Would you like a drink? *I* would."

Mama Girl got the bottle and poured one for Gladys and another for herself. Mama Girl was about to gulp hers down when Gladys held hers out, so they touched glasses, and then Gladys said, "To my best friend."

"Some friend!" Mama Girl said. "I've been treating you like a dog. I only hope your marriage is O.K., because that's the only thing that counts."

"It *really* is, isn't it?" Gladys said.

"Ten years ago I wish I knew what I know now," Mama Girl said. "Are you all right? Is Hobart all right?"

"Oh, yes. We're both just fine. And of course you know the big news."

"What news?"

"Didn't you tell her, Frog?"

"Tell her what?" I said.

"I'm going to be a mother."

Well, then Mama Girl and Gladys hugged and laughed, and then they both dried their eyes.

Mama Girl said, "I'm so glad for you, and I think it was awfully kind of you to come to Philadelphia."

"If we were *never* to speak again," Gladys said, "do you think for a minute I wouldn't see the first performance of *this* play?"

There was another knock on the door, and it was Mr. Mungo.

"We're having a meeting on stage in five minutes," he said.

"O.K.," Mama Girl said.

We took off our make-up and our costumes, and put on our street clothes.

Gladys said, "We're at the Benjamin Franklin. Please call us when you get home."

"We're there, too," I said.

"I know," Gladys said. "That's why *we* went there."

She and Mama Girl embraced quickly once more, and then Gladys went off, and Mama Girl poured one more drink.

"She's a real friend," she said. "A *real* friend."

We went onstage. The curtain was up, the auditorium was empty, only a little light bulb was shining on the stage, and everybody was there under the light. We knew how everybody felt, too. We stood with the other members of the cast and waited. At last Mike McClatchey stepped forward.

"Thank you very much, ladies and gentlemen," he said. "We have opened on schedule, and we have given our first performance. As professionals, that is all we have been *obliged* to do. Tomorrow evening we give our second performance. No matter what the critics say of the play, or of the performances, I know each of you will perform your part to the best of your ability. If the auditorium is half empty, if there are only *three* people out there, we will give the best performance we know how. You've all been under pressure, and you've worked hard. Even so, I'm sure you will understand that we must go on working. That is the reason we have a rehearsal onstage at one o'clock tomorrow afternoon. Thank you again, and good night."

Mama Girl and I walked away with the other members of the cast. Going down the backstage stairs Mama Girl stumbled, but she didn't fall.

"I'm drunk," she said.

We walked for two blocks. I held on to her real tight, because she couldn't walk straight.

"I'm sick and ashamed," she said.

I waved at a taxi and the driver drew up and opened the door. I helped Mama Girl in, and I helped her out, and up to our room. We got undressed, and then we got in our beds.

"I'd like to go to sleep and never wake up," Mama Girl said.

I listened to her in the dark until I knew she was asleep. Then I went to the phone and called Gladys.

"We've gone to sleep," I said. "We're both very tired."

I asked the hotel operator not to ring our phone until nine o'clock in the morning. I got back in bed, and went to sleep, but I kept doing the play all over again, the way I kept riding in the airplane after we had got to New York from California.

At nine in the morning the telephone rang and Mama Girl sat up in bed as if she had been struck by lightning. She looked very bad. She shook her head, and then she got out of bed and answered the phone. Then she just stood there, trying to remember, or maybe not to.

At last she telephoned room service and asked for coffee for her, and boiled eggs and chocolate and toast for me— and the morning papers.

When the waiter came up with the table she poured coffee into a cup and began to drink. She opened one of the papers and read the review, and then she opened the other one and read the review in that one, too.

She opened the eggs and put butter on top of them, and then she said, "They don't like the play."

"What do they know about anything?" I said.

"I forgot to call Gladys last night."

"I called her."

"Thank you, Frog. I was very unhappy last night."

"Don't be unhappy."

"Well, I tried. I did my best."

"We have a rehearsal at one."

"I know, and I wish we didn't. I wish there wasn't a performance tonight, either."

By noon all of the Philadelphia papers were out, and Mama Girl had read all of the reviews. Not one of the critics liked the play.

"They like the sets a little," Mama Girl said, "and the music. They like Mr. Mungo a little, too, but that's about all."

"I don't care," I said.

"Of course you care."

"No, I don't. *Honest* I don't."

"How can you *not* care?"

"Oh, I *care*, I guess, but I *don't,* too."

At one o'clock we were onstage.

Emerson Tully said, "I know we've all read the reviews and don't feel very much like working, but suppose we get to work just the same? Act One, then."

Chapter 28

Work and Work,
and Worry and Wait

*W*e began to work, and this time—for the *first* time—we *really* worked. We did little things over and over, because now Emerson and Mike and Miss Cranshaw *knew* where we had made mistakes.

When it was curtain time and I was onstage I could tell there weren't many people in the theater, but I was ready for that. When the curtain went up I saw that the orchestra was less than half full, but the balcony was packed. Those are the seats that don't cost so much. The people in the orchestra didn't like the play, but the people in the balcony did. Everybody in the play worked well—much better than last night—and we had at least as much applause at the end of the play as we'd had from a packed house last night. Mr. Mungo and Mrs. Cole and Mama Girl and I took our separate bow. When we got to our dressing room Mama Girl didn't pour herself a drink. She just took off my make-up, and then her own, and we got into our street clothes and left the theater. There was no meeting, but there was a message on the bulletin board. Rehearsal tomorrow at eleven in the morning.

The third night there were even fewer people in the orchestra, but again the balcony was packed, and the performance was the best yet. I did things on purpose in a way that seemed to be the right way, and so did everybody else, especially Mama Girl. The applause at the end of the play was the best so far, and the four of us took two bows instead of one. On the bulletin board was a message that said rehearsal would be at ten tomorrow morning.

On Saturday at the matinee the orchestra was packed—with women—and it was packed again at the evening performance—with men and women. There was a meeting onstage afterwards, and Mike McClatchey said, "We have come through the first week safely. The play gets better with every performance, but we are still far from home. Considering the reviews, the attendance has been quite good. I feel we should rehearse tomorrow, but I leave that to you. Mr. Mungo, will you find out the will of the cast?"

Mr. Mungo, who had been on the stage more than fifty years, glanced at each of us, and every one of us nodded.

"We want to work, Mr. McClatchey," he said.

"Thank you very much, ladies and gentlemen," Mike said. "Rehearsal at two, then, so that we can all sleep late or go to church. Good night, then."

Mama Girl and I walked home. At the hotel we bought the Sunday papers because Mama Girl said there might be second reviews of the play in them, but there weren't.

Monday evening the orchestra was less than half full, and for the first time so was the balcony. After the performance Mike McClatchey came to our dressing room, and after a few minutes he said, "I'm afraid we're going to have to close."

"I'm sorry, Mike," Mama Girl said. "I'm terribly sorry."

"I had counted on second reviews in the Sunday papers," he said, "and better attendance this week, but there it is—no money at the box office, and no money anywhere else."

"What about the backers?"

"They saw the first performance, they read the reviews, and they went back to New York. I've been on the phone every day with all of them. I can't even get them to come back and see the play again."

"Mike," Mama Girl said, "please don't misunderstand my saying this. I think if you were to get a name actress to play my part, matters would be a lot different."

"I could have had a name actress from the beginning," Mike said. "I wanted you."

"I haven't done the play any good. I've tried, and I'm going to go on trying, but let's face it, Mike, I'm not much of an actress."

"I've heard the same words from great actresses when they've been in a play the critics haven't liked," Mike said.

"Why haven't the critics liked the play?" Mama Girl said. "We *know* it's a good play—a fine play—maybe a great one. They haven't liked it because one of the big parts—mine—hasn't been *acted*. Oh, I've been *there*, all right. I've said my lines, but I *haven't* acted, Mike. After the first performance, before the reviews were out, I wanted to step out. I *would* have if there could have been somebody to take my place. I'm very sorry, Mike. I feel I've spoiled the chances of a fine play."

"You're entirely mistaken," Mike said. "You *are* an actress, and you've been doing your part expertly. I wouldn't have anybody else in the part."

"Well, thanks a lot," Mama Girl said.

"And I don't feel sorry at all," Mike said.

"If we *don't* close," Mama Girl said, "if we work hard, if we go to Boston for two weeks, will the play have a chance?"

"Ordinarily, under similar circumstances," Mike said, "I would say no, but with *this* play, and this cast, I *must* say yes. On the stage, even now, the play is a good play, but a play happens to an audience. We know we've failed with our audiences, but we haven't failed with *everybody* in every audience. There have always been a good number of people in every audience with whom the play *hasn't* failed. We know perfectly well the play is a good play, effectively staged and performed. It just hasn't gone with the majority of the people in our audiences *here*, that's all. That doesn't mean it won't go in Boston, or in New York. I think it will. We've all learned a lot, and we keep learning. The fact is that all we really need now is more money."

"Do you really think so, Mike?"

"I *know* so."

"How much do we need?"

"Oh, about twenty-five thousand, I'm afraid."

"That's a lot of money."

"Only when you need it and haven't got it," Mike said. "I'm still trying, of course. I haven't told anybody else we're closing, but I think they know anyway. I'm telling you, because I believed this play would launch your career as a fine actress, and I feel I've let you down."

"You can't possibly mean that, Mike."

"I believe it with all my heart," Mike said. "That's what I really came to tell you."

Mr. McClatchey smiled and nodded to Mama Girl, and then he said, "As for you, Twink, I've always tried not to produce plays with children in them, because I have four of my own—grown-up now, of course—and I wouldn't think of letting them appear in a play. Unfortunately, very important plays are frequently about children, and the only people who can play children are children. You were perfect for this part, and you have always performed it perfectly—not like a child, but like an artist. Thank you very much. In a few years, before you know it, you won't be a child any more, but you will always be an artist, and a real woman. Good night, both of you."

We took a taxi home, and there in the lobby were Gladys and Hobart.

"We've been waiting for you," Gladys said. "Let's go have a lot of ice cream."

We went to the dining room of the hotel, and each of us had a banana split. We talked about a lot of things, but most of all Gladys wanted to know from Mama Girl all about becoming a mother. After a while, though, she wanted to know how the play was going, and Mama Girl told her the truth.

"We've both seen it three times," Hobart said, "and we've liked it better each time."

"The critics *didn't* like it," Mama Girl said.

"They're awfully stupid," Gladys said. "Besides, it just *isn't* a Philadelphia play. It's a New York play."

"Well, it doesn't look as if New York will ever get to see it," Mama Girl said.

"Excuse me a minute," Gladys said suddenly.

She got up and left the dining room. She was gone about five minutes. Ten minutes later Mike McClatchey came to the table and sat down.

"I want to invest in the play," Gladys said.

"That's very kind of you," Mike said, "but I'm afraid nobody else does, and the play needs about twenty-five thousand dollars."

"I'd like to invest that much," Gladys said.

Mike McClatchey seemed confused. He had just met Gladys for the first time, and he didn't know what to make of her.

"I don't believe you," Mike laughed.

"I'll phone my lawyer tonight," Gladys said. "He'll be here tomorrow morning, and you and he can work out the details."

"They call backers of plays angels," Mike said, "but you're the first one I've ever met who looks like one, and what's more, *acts* like one."

"I didn't use to," Gladys laughed. "It's just lately, since my marriage."

"Of course, if the play's a hit, as I expect it to be," Mike said, "you stand to earn a fortune from your investment."

"I've always *had* a fortune," Gladys laughed, "but never the way I have it now."

"Oh?" Mike said.

"Yes," Gladys said. "I'm going to become a mother."

"I might add," Hobart said, "that when *she* becomes a mother I become a *father*. I feel fortunate, too."

We were all busy eating second orders of ice cream. We talked and talked, and then Mama Girl said, "We've got to get to bed."

We got up and went to our room, but we took our time about getting to bed.

"You're not sorry you're in the play, are you?" Mama Girl said.

"No."

"You're not mad at me for dragging you into it?"

"Oh, no."

"If the play's a hit, will you stay in it—maybe for six months in New York, maybe for longer?"

"I don't know. Do I *have* to?"

"Oh, no, Frog—you *don't* have to. Of course not. If you get tired of it, we'll just tell Mike, and he'll find somebody else to do it. He'll never find anybody to do it as well as you do, but he'll find *somebody*."

"I'll decide after we get to New York," I said.

"I'd never forgive myself if I felt I had made you do something you didn't really want to do."

"I know, Mama Girl."

The next evening we gave the best performance of all. Gladys and Hobart came backstage after the performance, and then there was a meeting onstage.

Mike McClatchey introduced Gladys and Hobart, and then he said, "The play goes to Boston for two weeks on schedule. It opens in New York at the Belasco on schedule. In the meantime, I have sent telegrams to every Philadelphia reviewer urging him to see the play again tomorrow night, even though new reviews won't do us any particular good in Philadelphia, as our run here is almost over. I just feel the critics owe it to themselves to see the play again. I think we've all improved, for one thing, but at the same time I think the critics missed the bus on opening night. I don't think we did. That *does* happen now and then. I have great confidence in the play, and in each of you. Thank you very much for your good work when things looked hopeless. That's the difference between professionals and amateurs."

Everybody was thrilled. All of the critics came to the performance the following evening, and then they wrote reviews in the papers the following day. Three of the reviews were good, but one of them was still bad. The man said he hadn't liked the play the first time, and he'd liked it even less the second.

Even so, the theater was packed at every one of the remaining performances.

Saturday night after our last performance in Philadelphia we all went straight from the theater to the train, and Sunday we were in Boston.

Chapter 29

A Bouncing Ball in Boston

*M*iss Cranshaw, Mama Girl, and I went to church in Boston Sunday morning, but we didn't go to a ball game afterwards, because there was a rehearsal at the Plymouth at two o'clock.

We went back to the Ritz after church, and there in the lobby was Gladys.

"Hobart had to stay in New York," she said, "but he's flying up soon."

We had lunch, and then walked to the Plymouth. Gladys sat out front with a pad and a pencil, to make notes. Mike walked up and down the center aisle, watching and thinking. Emerson Tully was all over the place. Sometimes he was onstage, sometimes in the orchestra, sometimes in the balcony. We never knew where he was going to be. All of a sudden we would hear his voice from far away.

"Hold it," he would say. "I can't hear you up here. Everybody please remember that this is a large theater, and so is the Belasco in New York. Our best friends are up here, so let's be sure they hear us."

Oscar Bailey worked in the pit, and Joe Trapp worked

with the stagehands and electricians on scene changes and lighting.

We all felt happy to be in Boston, in a new city, because it was like having a second chance. We rehearsed until seven, because it took that long to get through the whole play.

We took a break at five for half an hour, and Gladys read her notes about the play to Emerson, Mike, Miss Cranshaw, Oscar, Joe Trapp, Mama Girl, and me. Her notes were very sensible. Emerson himself said so. He asked her to please let him borrow them—for reference. Gladys and Mama Girl and I walked around the empty theater. We went to the lobby and looked around, and then we went backstage to our dressing room. They had coffee and I had a bottle of milk. They were glad they were friends again.

"If this play fails *now*," Mama Girl said, "I'll never forgive myself, because you've got a fortune in it."

"It's not *going* to fail," Gladys said. "Nothing is going to fail. It's always a matter of making up your mind, that's all. I made up my mind that my marriage wasn't going to fail, and it isn't. Of course I got a lot of help. Everybody *needs* a lot of help, and nobody ought to be unwilling to accept it."

"Well, I didn't help you any," Mama Girl said. "Who did?"

"Oh, yes, you *did* help me," Gladys said. "I didn't know you did at first, but I did later on."

"Well, all right if you say so," Mama Girl said. "Who else?"

"Well, Frog."

"Who else?"

"Kate."

"How did Kate help you?"

"First, she let me talk," Gladys said. "Then, she told me I was acting, which she said was the right idea only I was acting badly, and that was the reason I was having so much trouble. She told me how to act intelligently, and I've been doing it ever since. She said now that I was to become a mother it was time I began to act intelligently— like a woman, not like a spoiled girl. I was hurt at first, but got over it the minute I noticed how much better I felt when I acted intelligently. She told me to go home and be a wife to my husband, so I did. Hobart looked at me as if he were seeing me for the first time, and there wasn't anything silly about it, either. My marriage isn't going to fail, because I've decided I don't *want* it to."

"Well," Mama Girl said, "*you* certainly have grown up awfully quickly."

"Haven't *you?*" Gladys said.

"I'm afraid not. I'm working at it, though. And to be perfectly honest, I hate it. It bores me to death."

Gladys looked at Mama Girl, and then they both began to laugh.

"It's driving me crazy," Gladys said. "I don't want to act intelligently at all. I don't want to be a good wife. I don't want to have a child. I hate every bit of it, but what can I do? I'm stuck. It's really very sad. Sometimes I want to stamp my feet and scream and cry and throw things, but I can't anymore—I just can't, and it's killing me. Hobart's such a bore, and so am I, when I'm kind and intelligent. It's really terrible, but I've just *got* to go on acting intelligently, don't I?"

"Yes, you do," Mama Girl said. "Well, as they say, that's life."

"The *hell* it is!" Gladys said. "It's not life at all. It's something else, and I don't like it. I never have. I've always longed to be a part of life, but there just hasn't been any for me to be a part of. There *still* isn't."

I wasn't paying much attention to them. I was turning the pages of Mama Girl's scrapbook, full of photographs of us, and newspaper stories, and magazine articles. I was just half listening to the words they were saying. I knew from their voices that they were both happy, and that was the only thing that really mattered, but now I stopped looking at the scrapbook. I looked at them—the both of them. They were two little girls who were grown-up, but really *weren't*. They were thirty-three years old, but they still weren't really grown-up. They could talk and have fun, but deep inside they weren't happy.

"Well, what *is* life, then?" I said to Gladys.

"Oh, Frog!" Gladys said. "That's the trouble. I don't know. Nobody does. Not *really*. I guess that's what all the plays are about, all the novels, and operas, and symphonies, and paintings, and everything else. All those things happen because everybody wants to be a part of life, but doesn't know what life is. When you're little you think you'll know pretty soon—next year, or when you're sixteen, or surely when you fall in love and a boy goes crazy about you and kisses you—but even then you don't know. Even then it isn't really life, it's something else."

"What is it?" I said.

"More mistakes," Gladys said. "More confusion, more pain, more and more and more of the stuff you want to see changed. Oh, it changes, all right. It changes all the time, but always from bad to worse, never from good to better, or from better to perfect, unless you're a liar, unless you can fool yourself, which I have always tried to do, but never really have."

"Ah, you're crazy, both of you," I said.

Gladys and Mama Girl laughed happily and Gladys said, "You'll find out for yourself, Frog. Wait and see."

"I don't need to wait," I said. "I like things right now."

"Really?" Mama Girl said. *"Right now?"*

"Yes. Right now," I said.

"Do you like being in Boston, in a play?"

"Yes."

"Why?"

"Because I'm *in* Boston. *In* a play. Why shouldn't I like it?"

"Did you like it in *Philadelphia?"*

"Yes."

"Even when the opening night audience didn't like the play, or us? Even when the critics didn't say you gave a beautiful performance, which you did?"

"Yes, even then."

"But *why*, Frog? If you're telling the truth."

"Because I know I can't be doing what I'd rather be doing."

"What would you rather be doing?"

"Well, I always remember Macaroni Lane, and my friends there, and I think I'd rather be there, but I'm not, so I'm glad to be here, too. It's still *me*, it isn't somebody else."

"What else?" Mama Girl said.

"Most of all I'd rather be in Paris with my father and my brother."

"Doing what?"

"Just being there."

"Without me?"

"I'm *here* without my father," I said, "and I like it. I could be with him without you and like it, couldn't I?"

"I hate you," Mama Girl laughed. "You see," she said to Gladys, "what kids are."

"Best of all," I said, "I'd like all four of us to be somewhere together, in our own house, and then I'd like more of us—a little brother, and a little sister."

"Oh, you would, would you?"

"Yes, I would."

"Well, I'm sorry," Mama Girl said, "but I've been there before, and it just isn't for me."

"What *is* for you?"

"Never mind," Mama Girl said. "You know I don't know, so don't ask me. Whatever it is, it isn't *that.* And I think it's time we got back to work."

We went onstage and Gladys went back to her seat in the theater. Emerson Tully examined the notes Gladys had made, and we began to rehearse again.

We went through the rest of the play, and then Monday morning we began to go through the whole thing all over again.

I knew my part so well I could do it without thinking, but of course I couldn't stop thinking, because I saw Mr. Mungo and Mrs. Cole, who were the most experienced actors in the cast, working on their parts all the time. They tried new things out alone, and together. In the play Mrs. Cole was the grandfather's lady friend—she wanted him to propose to her, because she was lonely, and she knew he was, too. He was always nice to her, but he just wouldn't ask her to be his wife. She was always talking about his wife, who had been dead many years, and he was always talking about her husband, who had been his best friend, but had divorced her and gone away somewhere.

The rehearsal ended at four o'clock in the afternoon on Monday.

Everybody was excited and happy and confident.

The theater was packed Monday night, and we did the play.

Nobody forgot his lines, nobody did things badly, and the audience was very encouraging.

There were a lot of curtain calls, and for the first time Mama Girl and I took separate calls—three of them.

After the performance a lot of people from the audience came backstage, and everybody said the play was beautiful.

It was like a big family.

Mike McClatchey came to our dressing room, and then Emerson Tully, and Kate Cranshaw, and Oscar Bailey, and Joe Trapp, and Mr. Mungo, and Mrs. Cole.

Everybody said Mama Girl and I had really come through. They said that that was the reason the audience had liked the play.

The next day Mama Girl read the reviews in the Boston papers. Every review was good. Every review said Mama Girl was great. They said I had a long and difficult part, and did it well, but they said Mama Girl was on her way to being a star, and eventually a great actress.

She was stunned.

She and Gladys talked all about their childhood long ago.

After that it was easy for me to play my part every night, and in the afternoons on Wednesdays and Saturdays. It was nothing at all. Even if I said something another way, instead of the way I had *been* saying it, it was all right. It seemed as if I couldn't make a mistake.

One night when I thought I had made a lot of them, Mr. Mungo said I had given my best performance. I didn't feel captured any more, the way I *had* at first, with a hard job to do that I really didn't want to do, the way it had been in Philadelphia. I almost forgot the play itself, and what it meant. I had done my part so many times, and I knew it so well, it was like going for a walk and coming back and not remembering anything I had seen on the way—not even remembering I *had taken* a walk at all, because I had been thinking about other things all the time.

Mr. Mungo said to me one night as we were taking curtain calls—while the curtain was down—"I could learn a lesson from you in the art of acting, Twink."

The next time the curtain was down he said, "You act as if you weren't in a play at all, and I'm going to try to learn to do that, too."

He is a nice old man, and he dances backstage the way he used to in vaudeville when he was one of the biggest headliners. He seems so different then, so much younger, and so lively—the way he taps and turns, and says things, and sings. I'm certainly glad I met him.

The run in Boston was a success. Mama Girl and I were interviewed by a lot of newspaper reporters, and we were asked to go on different radio and television programs—to talk about the play and ourselves, and the others connected with the play.

The New York backers came up to Boston after they had read the Boston reviews. They asked Mike if they could put money into the play. He told them to speak to Gladys about it, because she owned the biggest piece of the play, after Mike. Gladys asked Mama Girl if she should sell some of her investment at a profit, and Mama Girl said, "Are you crazy? Of course not. If I were you I wouldn't even *talk* to them. I hated them at the party, and I hate them more than ever now. They are shameless. They've got their nerve asking you to sell some of your investment."

"Well," Gladys said, "I won't talk to them, then."

Writers and photographers from the big magazines, like *Life* and *Look,* came to Boston and talked to everybody and took pictures.

Emerson Tully, who had always worked so hard, began to drink, and he always seemed a little drunk. Even so, he worked every day. We kept right on trying to make the play better all through the Boston run. We didn't have full rehearsals anymore, but we *did* work on little parts of the play that Miss Cranshaw and Mike and Emerson believed ought to be improved. Every performance was a little different from the last one, and a little better, too.

One afternoon while Emerson was working with Mr. Mungo and Mama Girl he began to walk across the stage, and fell down. Mr. Mungo and Mama Girl tried to help him up but they couldn't. Mike McClatchey ran over and got Emerson on his feet, and then onto a chair. Emerson was very surprised.

Mike said, "Will somebody please get a doctor?"

But Emerson said, "No, Mike, I'm just drunk, that's all."

But Mike wouldn't let him get up and go back to work. Gladys ran to the phone and called Hobart, who had come up from New York, and after five or ten minutes Hobart came up on the stage and went to Emerson and began to examine him. Hobart used the stethoscope on Emerson. He took his pulse, and he turned a small light on his eyes.

After a while Hobart said to Mike, "Exhaustion."

"Are you sure?" Mike said. "That looked like an attack to me."

"I've been drinking a lot, that's all," Emerson said.

"Any particular reason why?" Hobart said.

"Yes," Emerson said. "This is my first play. I never expected to direct it. I've been drinking because I've been so tired and excited."

"Do you think you can stop feeling so much anxiety?"

"Not until we open in New York," Emerson said. "Why? What's wrong with anxiety? I'm twenty-seven years old. My whole reputation as a playwright is at stake. I don't want to stop being anxious until I have a right to."

"Mike," Hobart said, "isn't the play pretty much all right just as it is right now?"

"That's up to Emerson," Mike said. "It's his play, and he knows. He wrote a good play in the first place, and he's done a great job of directing. I don't know of anybody else who could have done as good a job. If he's up to it, I wouldn't want to *ask* him to stop."

"Well," Hobart said, "how about no more work *today*, then?"

"No, I'm O.K.," Emerson said.

"Better take the rest of the day off," Hobart said. "I'd like you to go home and forget all about the play. Have one more drink, maybe, and go to bed. Go to sleep. When you wake up have some soup and a steak. We'll see about tomorrow."

"Hell," Emerson said, "I'm not sick. I've just been drinking a little since the Boston reviews came out."

"All right, everybody," Mike said. "That's all for today. I'll be out front watching the performance tonight, the same as ever. I know it's going to be our best so far."

Everybody went away, but Mama Girl and I stayed. Oscar Bailey said to Emerson, "Look, I've been drinking a little, too. What do you say we take a slow walk back to the Ritz, and do what the doctor says?"

Oscar and Emerson left the theater together, and then Mike said to Hobart, "All right, let's have it."

"It appears to have been an attack all right," Hobart said, "but I didn't think I ought to tell him just yet. The fact is, he *is* exhausted, too, and I don't think he has been eating very much lately. He's going a little too fast, even for a man with a play to get to New York. I'll be looking in on him again later on, of course."

"Do you really want him to have one more drink?" Mike said.

"No, but I don't want him to be made sicker than he is by all sorts of quick changes. He's got to quiet down gradually. I have an idea that if I hadn't been called—if no doctor had—if he had fallen in private, so to say, he would have come out of it by himself. Mild attacks of this kind are a lot more frequent than most of us know. I had one myself at college, but of course I didn't know it at the time. He's got good basic health, but there's no point in placing too great a burden on it."

"He'll want to see the performance tonight," Mike said.

"I'd rather he didn't, but of course if he must, he must."

"Will you be giving him a sedative?"

"Hell, no," Hobart said. "That's for hysterical women."

Gladys looked at Mama Girl. She was angry, too, but Mama Girl only smiled.

"Are you sure he wasn't just drunk?" Mike said.

"I'm quite sure," Hobart said, "but it's nothing any of us can do anything about, not even a doctor, except to believe that he himself will look after himself. He'll find out for himself how to balance his own limitations with his own demands on himself, the same as we all do. I may say he's worked wonders with the play since Philadelphia. I saw it last night again, and I thought it was just about flawless. You've *all* worked wonders with it, but you've got to learn not to kill yourselves, too."

"Do you want to give us *all* checkups?" Mike said.

"Oh, no," Hobart said. "Everybody's just fine. Everybody's in perfect health."

"I've been having pains on top of my head," Mike said.

"So what?" Hobart said "You've been working hard. Forget it."

We all left the theater then and walked back to the Ritz. Gladys teased Hobart a little on the way about sedatives being for hysterical women, but she was glad he had come up from New York, and was her husband instead of her personal doctor, the way he had been for so long. *He* was glad about that, too.

We had only four more performances to give in Boston: that night, Friday night, Saturday matinee and evening, and then it was back to New York for all of us.

Emerson Tully didn't see the performance Thursday night, but he worked all day Friday, from ten in the morning to six in the evening. We ran through the whole play.

"It's our last chance," he said to all of us at ten in the morning. "We'll take it from the beginning, and we'll take our time. The play is getting stronger with every performance, and its values are beginning to be a lot more clearly defined, as they *should* be."

At the end of the last rehearsal he said, "Well, that's it until Monday morning at ten at the Belasco Theatre in New York. Sunday is going to be a holiday for all of us. Monday we're going to concentrate on sets and lights and music, and so for all practical purposes this has been our last rehearsal before the New York opening. I can only say to each of you—you have been great. You have worked hard. I consider it an honor to have you in my play, and to have worked with you. Thank you very much, ladies and gentlemen."

Saturday morning Emerson and Mike returned to New York, and that night after the last performance we all went straight from the theater to the train. Sunday morning we were back in New York.

Chapter 30

The Great Game

*M*ama Girl and I went back to the Pierre, but instead of going back to 2109 we took a much bigger room, with two beds in it.

On the train Mama Girl spoke to Miss Cranshaw about that, and Miss Cranshaw said, "The little room has served its purpose, but now you must have a larger room. If the play is a hit, it might be a good idea to move into an apartment somewhere, and make a real home."

"If?" Mama Girl said. "If the play is a hit? Isn't it going to be a hit?"

"It has an excellent chance," Miss Cranshaw said, "but of course no play is a hit in New York until it opens and has been reviewed. The first New York performance will tell the story. If we give a good performance—if the first-night audience *permits* us to give a good performance—if it *encourages* us to do so—then, I think the play will be a hit. I don't see how it could be anything else. The play has turned out much better than I believed it would. Emerson has done a fine job of creative directing."

"Is there anything more I ought to think about, or try to improve?" Mama Girl said.

"Absolutely not," Miss Cranshaw said. "Even if there

were, I wouldn't have you *trying* any more. Of course you will always try, and of course you must, but what I have tried to teach you is to *conceal* the trying, and you've managed to do that very effectively. Are you worried?"

"Scared to death," Mama Girl said. "I'll be right back," she said suddenly.

She got up and went away.

"How about you, Twink?" Miss Cranshaw said. "Are *you* worried?"

"Well, I want the play to be a hit," I said.

"Why?" Miss Cranshaw said.

"Why?" I said. "That's a funny question."

"No," Miss Cranshaw said. "Of course we all want it to be a hit, but what I want to know is why *you* do. You yourself."

"Because then everybody will be happy, and I like everybody better when they are happy."

"Any other reasons?"

"Well, if it's a hit, then after a while, if I want to, I can leave the play, and it won't be a mean thing to do."

"Oh?" Miss Cranshaw said. "You don't want to do a mean thing?"

"Oh, no."

"And you think you *may* want to leave the play?"

"I don't know for sure, but if it's a hit, and I *do* want to leave, then I'll know I can, and that's something I want to know."

"If you *do* leave the play, what will you do?"

"Nothing. I'll go to school, and play, and come home after school, and eat supper, and read, and look at TV. That's all. I *will* be able to leave the play if I want to, if it's a hit, won't I?"

"Oh, I think so, Twink," Miss Cranshaw said. "The part will have been set, and somebody else can be taught to do it, but I'm afraid nobody will ever be able to do it the way you do it."

"My friend Deborah Schlomb can do it better than I can."

"Oh, you think so? And who *is* Deborah Schlomb?"

"My best friend, in California. I know she can do it better than I can, because we always did plays, and Deb was always the best. She was the prettiest, and she knew how to act the best, too."

"What sort of plays did you do?"

"Plays Deb and I made up."

"Plays like our play?"

"Oh, no. More like Annie Oakley, where she stands on the horse and shoots with both pistols, and then captures the crooks."

"Well, perhaps if you decide to leave the play we ought to send for Deb."

"She wouldn't come."

"She wouldn't?"

"Oh, no. Her mother wouldn't let her."

"Why not?"

"Well, don't you see, they *live* there. All of them. Deb's father, and her mother, and her big brother, and her little brother, and her little sister. And they're going to have another one pretty soon, too. She wouldn't leave them to be in play when she is in plays of her own all the time, anyhow."

"Well, I suppose not," Miss Cranshaw said. "But then perhaps you won't want to leave the play."

"I don't know," I said. "It's fun, and I've met so many nice people I never even *knew* about before, but I know I don't want to be an actress when I grow up."

"No? Why not?"

"Just don't, that's all."

"What *do* you want to be?"

"Well, first a pitcher, of course. I want to pitch one real good season—oh, about twenty wins to only one or two losses, or maybe none. And then I want to get married and have a family."

"Pitching is acting, too, Twink."

"On a baseball field, though—in a game. A game that's different every time, with nobody needing to say anything about anything. Just get out there on the old sack and pitch. Or bat. Or field. Or throw. Baseball is beautiful."

"Our play is beautiful, too, isn't it?"

"Oh, yes, but of course I've never seen it, but when you are *in* it, it's the same every time."

"The audiences change."

"They do, and sometimes there is a *lot* of difference between one audience and another, like that audience we had a few days ago in Boston, where the man enjoyed the play so much all by himself. You remember the one. He knew exactly what we were doing, and every one of us acted better than ever. But in baseball *everybody's* like that one man in Boston. And the game is different every time. I want to pitch for the Giants. I want to pitch them to a pennant in the National League after they haven't had one for four or five seasons. None of the major leagues has got a girl pitcher."

"None of the minor leagues, either. They don't have a girl playing *any* position, for that matter."

"They *will*, though. I may be the first girl on a big-league ball club."

"You'll have to pitch awfully well," Miss Cranshaw said.

"Oh, yes," I said. "I've got to pitch much better than any boy, because they won't have me otherwise. I've got to be so good that they won't be able to afford *not* to have me."

"Have you been practicing?"

"Well, not very much lately—because I've been in the play."

"How do you practice when you *do* practice?"

"Oh, I get up on the old sack, and I stand there a minute looking at the batter and the catcher, and over at first in case there's a runner there, and then I take hold of the ball real tight, I wind up, and I pitch—a fast ball that's so fast they can't *see* it. If they're going to swing at all they've got to take a chance and swing anywhere. I pitch one a little high, another a little low, one in, one out, and all like that."

"*Where* do you practice, Twink?"

"Anywhere, but of course when my brother Peter Bolivia Agriculture was out there in the house on Macaroni Lane we used to practice in the back yard."

"Who?"

"My brother Pete. My father always liked to call him Peter Bolivia Agriculture. He's a good pitcher, too. He's maybe a little better than I am, but that's because he's older, I think. And of course he's been staying in shape in Paris, while I haven't. He's taught some Paris boys to play."

"You know, Twink, I don't doubt for a minute that some day you *will* pitch for the Giants. I don't doubt that you'll get married soon afterwards, either, and have a very wonderful family."

Mama Girl came back and she said, "All right, Frog, it's after midnight. I think we'd better get to sleep."

All day Sunday we just loafed in our new room at the Pierre, number 3132. Mama Girl talked on the telephone almost all day. She even called Clara Coolbaw in California.

Clara said my goldfish were just fine, and of course she
and Mama Girl talked about everything under the sun.
Mama Girl said Clara just *had* to take an airplane and
come to New York. Clara asked Mama Girl to hold the
line, and she asked her husband if she could do that, and
he said she couldn't, but late in the day Mama Girl
received a telegram from her, and Clara said: ARRIVE NEW
YORK ONE O'CLOCK MONDAY AFTERNOON. SEE YOU AT THE
PIERRE AT TWO OR THREE. LOVE. Mama Girl was thrilled,
because now her two best friends would be out front to see
her on opening night: Gladys Dubarry Tuppence, and
Clara McGuire Coolbaw. McGuire was Clara's name before she married Sam Coolbaw, who is a real-estate and
insurance agent.

"You've called everybody in the world," I said. "How
about letting me call a few people?"

"Who would you *like* to call?" Mama Girl said.

"You know who."

"Who?"

"My father, that's who."

"Well, all right, Frog," Mama Girl said. "Call your
father."

I took the phone and gave the hotel operator my father's number in Paris, and after about half an hour she
called back and said there was no answer, should she try
again in twenty minutes? I said yes, but there was no
answer twenty minutes later, either. She kept trying for a
long time, and then Mama Girl said, "Well, I guess they've
taken a weekend trip somewhere."

Late Sunday afternoon Mama Girl and I went out and
hired a horse and carriage, with an old man in uniform
driving. We drove all around Central Park. It was very
expensive, but we didn't care.

"We're entitled to a little luxury," Mama Girl said.

"We've worked hard, amid tomorrow night we have got to give the best performance of all."

"Are you scared *now*, the way you were before we even started to read for Miss Cranshaw?"

"Oh, no," Mama Girl said. "I'm scared, but not *that* way anymore."

"What way, then?"

"I'm afraid of the kind of audience we're going to have, because if it isn't a good one, if it doesn't fall in love with the play the minute the curtain goes up, we are going to have a hard time—and maybe a flop instead of a hit. The play *is* a hit. The question is, is our audience going to be a hit, too. Are you scared, Frog? Tell the truth."

"The *real* truth?"

"Of course."

"The absolute real positive truth?"

"Oh, come on, Frog."

"I'm *not* scared."

"And you're *not* worried about the opening-night audience?"

"No."

"Suppose they're awful? New York opening-night audiences generally are. They arrive late. A lot of them are drunk. Most of them have had too much dinner and they're uncomfortable. They aren't even really interested in the play. Suppose they're awful?"

"Let 'em be. We'll just do our work and go home."

"Frog," Mama Girl said, "tomorrow night Gladys is giving a big party at her house for the whole cast. We're all going to be staying up until the morning papers are out. That's not until after three, and then if the reviews are good, and we've got a hit, then of course nobody is going to want to hurry away. I mean, we're going to want to stay up and celebrate."

"That's good," I said. "After the play, I'll go home and go to sleep. I won't be afraid."

"Oh, no. That isn't what I mean, Frog. Gladys wants you and me to spend the night, so of course you'll be at the party, too—until midnight at least, and a little later if you feel like it. I mean, if it's a hit, shall I wake you up and tell you?"

"Just wake me up *a little*. Just say yes, and I'll know. But if it isn't a hit, don't wake me up, even a little."

"All right, but you *do* feel it's going to be a hit, don't you?"

"Yes, I do."

"Are you glad?"

"Very."

"Why?"

"Miss Cranshaw asked the same question. I'll be glad it's a hit because you will be in a fine play for a long time. You will be earning a lot of money. You will be famous. And I will be able to leave the play if I want to."

"Are you *going* to want to?"

"I don't know yet, but I think I will after a while."

"What do you want to do instead?"

"Nothing, Mama Girl."

"I thought you might want to go to Paris."

"Do you want me to?"

"If the play is a hit and you want to leave, and you want to go to Paris, I want you to."

"If it isn't a hit?"

"Then of course I don't want you to go."

"Why if it is, and why not if it isn't?"

"Because if it isn't, I'd be lost without you, that's why, and you know it."

"Then, if it's a hit and I want to leave, I want to go to

Paris, but if it isn't, then I don't want to go. I don't want to leave you."

"You're my friend, Frog."

"What'll we do if it isn't a hit?"

"Oh, let's not think about it."

"No, Mama Girl, what *will* we do?"

"Well, I don't know about you, but I'll kill myself."

"How?"

"How? Is that all you've got to say?"

"Oh, Mama Girl, I know you're just talking, but if you really wanted to—if *anybody* did, how would they do it?"

"Sleeping pills are what a lot of crazy women have been taking lately."

"They *are* crazy, aren't they?"

"Of course they are, but I feel sorry for every one of them just the same."

"Have *you* ever thought of taking them, Mama Girl? I mean, just thought of it?"

"Oh, yes, Frog. I might as well come clean. When things were very bad between your father and me, before we got divorced, I thought of it quite a lot, but not as much as I did afterwards."

"Afterwards? When?"

"When we were home. When all I did was go to parties."

"I thought you liked parties."

"I did, but only because they helped me get through a little more time—a little more useless, dead time. But whenever I got home at two or three or four or five in the morning—whenever I was alone again, and all keyed up about nothing—about nothing at all, Frog—I thought a lot about taking them."

"Did you have some to take?"

"Yes."

"Where are they now?"

"I took them."

"You did *not.*"

"One at a time, the way they're *supposed* to be taken, beginning in Philadelphia. Now they're all gone."

"Don't you ever buy any more."

"All right."

The driver of the carriage took us to the door of the Pierre on Fifth Avenue. We got out, Mama Girl paid him, and then she gave him a very big tip—three dollars—he thanked her, and we went inside.

There were a lot of phone messages for Mama Girl in the box for 3132, but they weren't important. We went upstairs, and I tried to get my father on the phone in Paris again, but again there was no answer.

We had supper in our room, we looked at TV, and then I went to bed, but Mama Girl just sat there in the dark, still looking at TV.

Chapter 31

It's a Hit, It's a Flop, It's a Hit, and Who Cares?

I'll never forget the New York opening. The curtain was supposed to go up at half past eight sharp, but it didn't, because a lot of important people hadn't reached the theater yet, especially two big critics.

Mike McClatchey kept looking through a little hole in the curtain at the audience. He knew where the critics were supposed to sit, but their seats were still empty at a quarter to nine.

"It would be just my luck if they were both killed in taxi accidents," he said.

Emerson Tully kept walking up and down, all alone.

"The expectant father," Kate Cranshaw said, and then Emerson stopped and looked at her as if he hadn't ever seen her before.

Mr. Mungo danced and sang one of his songs from vaudeville long ago. "I knew you when I saw you, Rose of the Bowery. Who wouldn't know you, Rose, red and flowery?"

Mrs. Cole said, "Thank God for one more New York

opening night. I haven't felt so young in twenty years. Young, and *shattered.*"

Mama Girl turned the pages of the program, which is something like a magazine, full of advertisements, and read the notes about the cast.

"Everybody in the play, except you and me, Frog, is famous," she said. "Mrs. Cole did Shakespeare when she was your age, and she was world-famous long before she was my age."

"We *should* go up," Mike said, "but we can't. "We've *got* to wait for those two critics."

Joe Trapp went around checking up on everybody—costumes, make-up, set, props, and everything else.

Telegrams kept arriving for everybody, even me. Mine were from everybody connected with the play, even Helen Gomez. She stayed near Mike McClatchey, to help him keep track of everything, to remind him of things, to be somebody for him to talk to. She was all dressed up, and she looked young and pretty.

"What time is it now?" Mike said.

"Ten to nine," Helen said.

"We've *got* to go up, that's all."

"No, the audience doesn't mind. Everybody out there is having fun. Wait for the critics."

"Forever?"

"They'll be here."

Emerson went to Mike and Helen, and took a peek through the hole in the curtain at the audience.

"They're awfully jittery," he said. "They're jumping around. They look like a bad audience to me."

"Not at all," Helen said. "They're the best audience we could ever hope for."

"They're not interested in the play," Emerson said. "They're interested in themselves."

"Now, you stop worrying," Helen said. "I've seen a lot of opening-night audiences, and the time to worry is when you've got a glum, silent one. This audience is just fine."

"They're *not* interested in the play, though."

"They haven't *seen* it yet."

"Well, if we don't go up soon," Emerson said, "they never will. And they won't mind at all. As far as they're concerned, *they* are the play. Next play I write, Mike, the curtain goes up at nine for five minutes. Two or three people on the stage are sitting somewhere, doing nothing, saying nothing. It goes up again for five minutes more—nothing on the stage again—just a few people, sitting around, reading, looking at things, not saying anything. It goes down for another forty-five minutes, so the audience can go back to having fun, living in the theater. It goes up for Act Three, which is only *three* minutes. The climax is a big sleepy dog that comes on stage, looks at the people, gets discouraged, and lies down and goes to sleep—beside a cat. That's going to be my next play. The hell with any silly play that makes demands on the people who come to the theater. I'll write a play they'll love. I've nearly killed myself trying to get this play in shape for New York, but look at them, will you? No play in the world could hope to compete with *them*. So this is New York. I should have been born in a small town somewhere."

"Here they are," Mike said.

He waved at the electrician, who pressed a button, and the overture began.

Then Mike put his arm around Emerson, and they came to where the rest of us were.

"All right," Mike said. "This is it, ladies and gentlemen. The audience is healthy. The critics are all in their seats. I know they are going to love you, just as I do. I know you are going to give the performance we have all been working for—the *first* New York performance. Good luck."

I went on stage, and Mr. Mungo waited in the wings. Mike turned to the stagehand who took care of the curtain. He lifted his arm, and then after a moment the overture ended. Mike waited a moment, and then he brought his arm down, and the stagehand took the curtain up, and there I was alone on the stage.

There wasn't an empty seat in the whole theater. I couldn't *see* that there wasn't—I could feel it. I knew Gladys and Hobart were in the first row, and that Clara Coolbaw was across the aisle from them, with her husband— she'd made him come to New York, too. I didn't know anybody else in the audience, but whoever they were, they quieted down very quickly.

When the curtain first went up, there was a kind of rush from out there to the stage—a rush of people, or heat, or excitement. And sound, too. It wasn't a sound of talking. It was a sound of breathing, or of a lot of people being packed together out there side by side from the bottom of the place to the top. It was a sound of silence of some sort, of people quickly not talking anymore. There were sounds of seats, too—of people moving a little in them, or of sitting in them, and there were little flashes of light as ushers moved down the aisles silently getting the last arrivals to their places.

For a whole minute or two I had nothing to say or do on the stage, except look out a window, turned away from the audience. And then, whenever I thought it was time to do so, I was supposed to hum and sing a little—I could hum, *or* sing, or just half sing, because Emerson said he wanted me to do it any way I wanted to.

"The softer the better," he said in Boston.

And then I was supposed to turn away from the window

and look around the whole room, which was a poor one, in a poor house, early in the evening, and nobody else home. I had a red-and-white rubber ball about twice as big as an orange that was a little punctured, so it didn't bounce very well. I was supposed to pick it up, look at it, and then practice bouncing it, but not really bounce it. And then I was supposed to bounce it—but of course it didn't really bounce. All it did was make a soft sound, and hardly bounce at all.

But immediately afterwards things happened to that place. The walls moved away, and beyond them was a whole different place, full of light. My imaginary friends began to be there, only they couldn't be seen—but their voices could be heard. We talked and heard music and danced and sang. Then I heard footsteps, and I knew it was my grandfather, Mr. Mungo.

Well, in order to get the place back the way it really was I had to bounce the ball again, only I couldn't find it. Mr. Mungo came in and looked around, and he wanted to know what had happened to everything. I said everything was the same as ever, wasn't it? I found the ball, bounced it, and then very quickly everything *was* the same as ever. Mr. Mungo put his hand on his forehead. He thought maybe something was the matter with him. We had a talk, and after a moment Mr. Mungo said the older he got the nearer he got to his own childhood—was I sure things hadn't been different when he had first come in? He promised not to tell anybody, to keep it a secret, so I told him the truth. He examined the ball, which he had given me for a birthday present long ago. He bounced it, but nothing happened, so he asked me to bounce it. I said I didn't know if it would work when I wasn't alone, but I'd try.

I took the ball and thought about my friends, and then

I bounced it, and everything changed. Mr. Mungo brought his big watch out of his vest pocket and looked at it. He said we had half an hour before my mother would get home from work.

So we were together in that different place, with my friends.

And then one of Mr. Mungo's friends came in—only she came *walking* in.

She was a girl he had known when he was seventeen and she was fifteen—and she had died, but here she was just as pretty as she had ever been, and Mr. Mungo an old man now. I liked her very much, but I wanted to know why my friends couldn't come in, *too*. Mr. Mungo said they needed time. Her name was Rose, and she could dance and sing better than anybody in the whole world, and just to hear her speak made you feel happy to be alive. *Still* alive, Mr. Mungo said. When it was time for her to go, we both felt sad, and Mr. Mungo blew his nose and dried his eyes.

Everything went very nicely straight through the whole first act. Mama Girl came home in her tired clothes, but of course we had already bounced the ball, and so the place was the same as ever. We talked while Mama Girl tidied up the place, because she always kept busy. We talked about the weather and the neighbors and what we'd have for supper and about Mr. Mungo's son, who was Mama Girl's husband, and my father—but he had gone away years ago. Nobody knew where he was. And then Mama Girl picked up a little green handkerchief that Rose had dropped, and she wanted to know whose it was. Mr. Mungo and I looked at each other, and then he said it was his friend's—Mrs. Cole's. Mama Girl handed it to him, and laughed, and a lot of other things happened, and then it was the end of the first act.

The applause almost scared me, it was so loud. We had never heard applause like that before, not even at the *end* of the play, so when we went to our dressing room Mike and Emerson and Kate and Helen Gomez came there, and they said the play was going great, better than ever, and then Mike asked Helen to please get out among the intermission people and listen carefully to what they were saying. Just before it was time for the curtain to go up again Helen came back and said, "They *love* it, that's all. They just love it."

In the second act Mama Girl bounced the ball accidentally, and it worked for her, too. After a while Mr. Mungo's son came there, and Mr. Mungo began to cry, almost like a small boy. At first I didn't know why, but after a while I knew it was because his son was dead, and then I *almost* cried, too—but I wouldn't let myself do it. Because he was my father, and he was dead, and he and I were too proud to cry.

My father looked at me, and I looked at him, and then instead of running to him, I went and stood beside him, and he took my hand. He said he had to go now, so I said I wanted to go with him. This made Mama Girl almost go crazy. She grabbed me away from him, and she hollered at him, and bounced the ball, but it didn't work. And the rest of Act Two I wouldn't bounce the ball to make him go away, so then he knelt down and looked at me, and he spoke to me very softly, and then he got up and took the ball and bounced it himself, and everything changed back to what it had been—and he was gone, and he took the ball with him.

The applause this time was even louder than the first time, and everybody backstage was thrilled.

In the last act Mr. Mungo and I tried to find some other way to get Rose to come back, but no matter what we tried, it didn't work. Mr. Mungo got sick and had to lie down all the time. Mrs. Cole came by to keep him company, and ask him to get better and be her husband, like a sensible man of seventy-seven, but Mr. Mungo said things she couldn't even understand, even when he talked about her husband, who had been his friend, and she talked about his wife, and then after a while she went home. Mr. Mungo and I tried some more, but it didn't work. He gave me half a dollar to go and buy a ball like the one my father had taken away.

While I was gone a man visited Mr. Mungo, but he *really* visited him—knocked at the door, and came in like anybody, only he *wasn't* anybody. He was a nice man, and he said to Mr. Mungo that it was time Mr. Mungo turned over and went to sleep, but Mr. Mungo said he wanted just a little more time, because his granddaughter had gone to fetch something for him, something very important, and so the man said all right, then, and he went away. When I got back with the new ball that was like the one we had had, only new, Mr. Mungo took it and looked at it, and thought about it, and then he handed it to me and asked me to please bounce it, so after a minute I did, but nothing happened, and we both felt very bad. So then the man knocked, and Mr. Mungo turned and looked at the door, and then he called out to the man to come in, and the man came in very slowly. He smiled at me, and then at Mr. Mungo, and he took the ball and he began to bounce it. At last he looked at Mr. Mungo and he said it was time, but Mr. Mungo said he was afraid. He needed somebody out of his life to be with him—his childhood sweetheart, Rose.

"All right, then," the man said, and he bounced the ball, and this time it worked. Everything changed, and there she was again. Mr. Mungo sat up, and she went to him and took him by the hand.

"Shall we go?" the man said. Mr. Mungo got up and said good-by, and he and the beautiful girl and the man went away.

From far away the man tossed the ball back into the room, like an infield fly, and on the first bounce everything began to change back. I got the ball and began to bounce it, to keep everything the way it was, but it didn't work. Everything got dark, and then after a minute everything was the same as ever, and there in the corner of the room was Mr. Mungo lying on the couch, with his face to the wall. I went to him, but he didn't turn around. I shook him and tried to turn him around, but I couldn't. Mama Girl came in. She looked at me, and then she looked at Mr. Mungo, and then she just sat down.

"Your grandfather's dead," she said. We didn't cry or anything. We just sat at the little table, and just looked at each other. Then Mama Girl really came to her big chance to act. She sent me to get Mrs. Cole, and while I was gone she took the ball and bounced it, and this time nothing changed. It was night now, and the place was dark, and then Mr. Mungo came back, and then his son, and the three of them talked. They wanted Mama Girl to go with them, but Mama Girl said she wouldn't go. She got out her bankbook, to see how much money she'd saved, and then she began to count the money she had in her purse, and in a teapot, and in a piggy bank that she broke, and she got all of it counted, while she talked to them, and began to put things in a suitcase for her and me. When she was ready she went to them, and turned them both around, and pushed them gently out the door, and they went away.

When Mrs. Cole and I went back the place was very

dark, so Mrs. Cole switched on a light, and then she went to Mr. Mungo on the couch and she took his hand and held it, and Mama Girl said she and I were going away now. She said she would stop at the undertaker's around the corner and pay them, and she and I would be at the funeral day after tomorrow, but now we were going away. She said Mrs. Cole could keep the furniture—she didn't want it anymore. So Mama Girl and I went away, and then it was just Mr. Mungo and Mrs. Cole. She saw the ball on the floor and she picked it up and ran after us, to give it to me, but we were gone. She went back and just dropped the ball, and then everything began to change again, only brighter and more beautiful than ever, and the curtain came down and the play was over.

Somebody said we took seventeen curtain calls. Three were for Mama Girl and me alone, and then three more were for Mama Girl alone, and then some people began to shout "Author," so Mike McClatchey made Emerson Tully go out and take a bow. The minute he was out there, everybody stopped applauding, so he could say something.

Emerson said, "This is my first play. I feel very fortunate in the people who have performed it, and in the people who have seen it. Thank you very much." He ran off then, and the audience applauded louder than ever. Mike and Kate Cranshaw sent Emerson back with the whole cast, and we took a few more bows, and that was the opening night.

Of course I didn't see the play, so I don't know what it was like out front. I liked the way Oscar Bailey played the music, though, and the way Mr. Mungo and Mrs. Cole talked, and the way Agnes Hogan, who played Rose, danced and sang, and the way Mama Girl did her whole part.

Backstage at the Belasco was a wild place for a long

time. It seemed as if everybody in the theater came backstage. There were all kinds of telegrams waiting for Mama
Girl when we got to our dressing room, and the room was
full of flowers, too, but she was too excited to open the
envelopes and read the telegrams, or to find out who had
sent the flowers.

"Well, that's it, Frog. What do you think of the play?"
Mama Girl said.

"I like it all right, but where do they go?"

"Who?"

"The mother and the daughter when they leave there—in
the play."

"They go—somewhere else."

"Is that all?"

"Well, the point is that in spite of everything—in spite
of the terrible unattractiveness of the world they live
in—they go on. They keep trying."

But then everybody began to pile into the dressing
room: Mr. Mungo and Mrs. Cole and Agnes Hogan, and
then Mike McClatchey and Emerson Tully and Oscar
Bailey and Joe Trapp and Helen Gomez, and then Gladys
and Hobart, and Clara and Charley—and it was a
madhouse.

At last we got out of there, though, and we took a taxi
to Gladys's house, and the party began. There was everything there to eat and drink—but mainly champagne and
big buckets of caviar.

At midnight I got tired of the noise and excitement, so
I asked Mama Girl to take me to my room. We went up to
the penthouse and I got in my bed, and Mama Girl sat on
the bed and she said, "Frog, you are my friend—my only
friend. Don't think I don't know what you've done for
me."

"I haven't done anything, Mama Girl."

"Not much you haven't," she said. "Just *everything*. I don't know what you really think of the play, and I don't know how you really feel about being in it, but I know you've given me my big chance."

"I like the play all right," I said. "At first I liked it very much. I thought it was the most beautiful play I had ever heard about, but now I think I'm a little tired of it. The same thing over and over again—not like baseball at all. I want to pitch."

"I know," Mama Girl said.

"But you don't think I ever will, do you?"

"I didn't say that."

"It's what you think, though."

"No, it isn't."

"Well, I *am* going to pitch. I know I am. Plays are about people, and people are always in trouble—people trouble. Baseball games are about baseball and baseball players, and somebody's always in trouble, but at the same time somebody else isn't, and it's a game, and after the game you go to the showers and shave with Gillette blades and then smoke a Chesterfield or a Camel, and then maybe drink a bottle of Budweiser or Schlitz, and the next day there's a new game. I just want to pitch until I lose my arm, and then I just want to get married and have my children."

"Of course, Frog. You go to sleep now, and dream your beautiful dreams."

"Don't forget to wake me up a little and say yes if it's a hit."

"All right."

"Because if it is, I want to leave the play as soon as I can, and I want to go to Paris."

"All right, Frog—and thank you very much again."

Mama Girl shut off the light and I thought about

pitching for the Giants in ten or eleven years, and I pitched real great. I was fast asleep when somebody kissed me on the cheek and said, "Yes." Well, it *was* a hit, then. The play was a hit, and so I could leave it and go to Paris, but that wasn't Mama Girl. Who was it? Or was I dreaming? I sat up and opened my eyes.

And there was my father, so I *knew* I was dreaming, and then I woke up, I was wide-awake, but it was *still* my father.

"Yes, Twink, it's me."

We hugged and kissed, and I said, "Where's Peter Bolivia Agriculture?"

"It's almost four o'clock in the morning," he said. "He's fast asleep."

"When did you get here?"

"Just in time to see the play. Mike McClatchey held the curtain for us."

"Did you like the play?"

"I liked *you* in it, Twink."

"Did you like Mama Girl?"

"Yes, I liked Mama Girl, too."

"Is it a hit?"

"Well, so far it looks like it's a *big* hit."

I jumped out of bed and began to jump up and down and holler, "Yay."

"Well, it looks as if you're going to be very famous and very rich."

"Very famous and very rich?" I said. "Didn't Mama Girl tell you?"

"Tell me what?"

"I'm not staying in the play."

"You're *not?*"

"Oh, no. Mama Girl's staying. I'm going to Paris with you and Peter Bolivia."

"No fooling?"

"No fooling. Because I'm a pitcher. I'm not an actress."

"O.K., Twink. Now, go back to sleep."

I got back in bed, and my father sat there beside me, and we talked very softly, and then I fell asleep.

I went out on the old sack. The catcher threw me the ball. I took a tight hold on it, and then I let it go—it was a fast ball that was so fast the batter didn't even see it.

I pitched three strikes each to three batters, and retired the side.

Afterword

Lucy Saroyan

*M*ama I Love You is a book written by my father, William Saroyan, for me, about me, dedicated to me, and it originally even had my photo on the back of the dust jacket. I was nine when it was published, and it was the most exciting thing that had happened to me so far. It came to be because my brother, Aram, and I would plead with our father to tell us stories whenever he visited us. Our parents were divorced. We spent our weekends and summers with Papa—but since he lived close by he often dropped in on weekday evenings for dinner and bedtime, That's when we would ask him to tell us stories. And after one story we'd want another, then another. He made them up on the spot and they were great. We couldn't get enough of them. But one night he announced that since we were both good readers it was no longer appropriate for him to tell us stories when he preferred us to read stories in books. However, he softened this bad news with a promise. He would write a whole book for each of us. Our very own books that we could read over and over. Mine came first, no doubt because he loved me more—at least he said he did each time I asked who his favorite was, which was at least three times a week. He always accompanied this answer with a roar of laughter and maybe even a wink at my irritated older brother. Nevertheless, my book came first. Aram's book came a year later and was called *Papa You're Crazy.*

When I say that the book is "about me" I don't mean that all the details of the story are true. Mama and I did not move into the Pierre Hotel, nor did I star in a Broadway play—but the details of the characters are us. The personality of Twink is exactly how I was at the time, and Mama Girl, and the other characters as well, are real people, we know—just with fictional names. My father always said you can only write about what you know. And he sure knew us. Of course, in the book we're all just a little sweeter and more interesting but essentially the same, just without the tiresome aspects.

One difference I was grateful for is that in the book my father's nickname for me is Twink. In real life my nickname was Tumbleweed, because I moved swiftly and in random directions, but by the time I was nine this didn't seem suitable in my opinion (although now, decades later, I love the name Tumbleweed, which is all through the letters my father wrote me). There was a girl in my class at school who was almost twelve—she'd been left back several times—and I found her very grown-up and fascinating. Her nickname was Twink. So at home I made reference to "Twink this, Twink that"—openly admiring her nickname. It's lucky for Papa that he didn't wait any longer to write the book, because shortly after its publication, a family moved to our neighborhood, and the girl my age was addressed by her family and friends as Princess. This was a shock to all the neighborhood kids. We were not at all sure whether this meant she *really* was a princess or not. It took a few weeks, but we discovered in no uncertain terms that she wasn't—but that's another story. In any case Princess replaced Twink as my favorite nickname for a while.

Some of the things that are exactly true are: I planned to be a pitcher for the New York Giants when I grew up, I never liked to eat, we lived in Pacific Palisades (at 1008 Maroney Lane, not 1001 Macaroni Lane), my best friend was Deb, and I was always catching frogs, ladybugs, anything I could catch—but I always let them go. My favorite thing in the whole world was to watch my mother get dressed up. From start to finish. The minute the bathroom door opened and the steam and perfume wafted into the hall I would bolt into the bathroom and join my mother as she began her ritual, wrapped in a towel. The rules were strict; I was not allowed to talk or to touch anything. I sat on the top of the toilet seat and watched her image in the mirror as she turned from milky white and pale pink into brighter colors. Then we moved to her room, where she had already laid out her clothes, and as she assembled the finishing touches it seemed to me there could be no one more beautiful and glamorous in the world. But, believe me, the sitting still and being quiet weren't easy.

The original title of the book was *I Love You, Mama Girl*, but it was too long for the book jacket, so it was shortened. I did call her Mama Girl, but I always just called my father Papa.

Certain things *like* the incidents in the book happened, but not with the same outcome, Once I was asked by a friend of my mother's to play a part on television. The part was about a little girl with eleven fingers—six on one hand, five on the other. The play was called *The Rope Dancers*, and it was a good part. I read it, Mama read it, and then we sent it to Papa for final approval. In this case he refused permission, asking how in the world could a little girl with ten fingers understand how a girl with eleven would feel without actually being a professional actress? I was disappointed, but in a way I was also relieved, because I thought some people might actually believe forever that I had six fingers on one hand, and was still young enough to worry about it.

The most real thing about the book is that it *feels* like my family was at that time. Rereading it I hear our voices, our special way of communicating with each other, our special way of loving each other very much, even though we didn't live together. At least, we didn't live with Papa. One of the best things about the book was that in "my story" Aram stayed pretty much out of the picture, but in reality we both lived with our mother unless it was a weekend or summer, in which case we both lived with our father. So just in story form it was fun to have my mother all to myself. Know what I mean? If you have a brother, I bet you do.

My father died in 1981, and I miss him every day. When he gave me the first copy of *Mama I Love You* along with the dedication, he also inscribed it to me. He wrote: "Lucy, Darling, I wrote this story for you. I hope you like it and I hope some day you will write a story for me." I regret that he did not live to read a story for him from me. But if I ever write it, I will call it: *Papa I Love You.*

August 1987